MY BLAQUE THEATER
A THEATER ANTHOLOGY

MIZ PORTIONTÉ FLOES
©2024

MY BLAQUE THEATER
A THEATER ANTHOLOGY

TABLE OF CONTENTS

THE DAILY SKITZ SERIES PG 4

- *WHAT YOU NEED 2 DO IZ*
- *DINNER WITH RICK'S MOM*
- *SHOPPING ADVICE*

I AINT IN YOUR SHADOW... YOU IN MY LIGHT! PG 17

HE'S MASSA'S BREEDER PG 39

ROYALTY REVISITED PG 64

4 JAZZY SOULZ PG 99

ONCE UPON A JAZZY SOUL AT THE JAZZY SOUL CAFÉ PG 123

ONCE UPON A JAZZY SOUL AT THE JAM PG 140

ONCE UPON A JAZZY SOUL ER BODY N DA CLUB PG 162

JAZZY BLUEZ ALL UP IN MY SOUL PG 200

THIS PAGE IS UNAPOLOGETICALLY BLANK

DAILY SKITz

WHAT YOU NEED TO DO IZ...

                NARRATOR:

Hey friends, this skit begins with Tish on a virtual coffee conference with her 2 besties

Tish is currently in a relationship with her boo Rick. Occasionally Tish will organize a coffee conference with her besties to vent about whatever issue she is having with Rick. In essence; allowing her girls in on all the business. Yet the conference is always disguised as a dish the dirt with the girls. Yet Tish doesn't really care how or what is going on in their lives. It's usually nothing anyhow. They are single and getting little to no action. Let's watch / listen.

                TISH:

(SITTING AT HER CAFÉ TABLE SIPPING COFFEE AND STARING AT HER IPAD SPEAKING WITH HER 2 BESTIES)

Grand rising Queens! Everybody got their java and ears ready?

(she perks her lips and widens her eyes)

                RITA:

(SITTING JUST OUTSIDE OF THE NIEGHBORHOOD CAFÉ TABLE SIPPING COFFEE AND STARING AT HER TABLET SPEAKING WITH HER 2 BESTIES)

YAAASSS! HONTY! The latte is hot, and ears are perky and in listening position.

(she laughs and snaps her fingers)

CAMMI:

(SITTING IN HER BED BLOWING HER HOT MUG OF COFFEE, LIGHTING A BLUNT AND STARING AT HER CELL PHONE SPEAKING WITH HER 2 BESTIES)

> Ready to wake, bake, and intake some drama from one of my lil mommas. Batter up! Who's 1st to dish the dirt?

RITA:

(places her coffee cup on the table and looks into the tablet screen with a serious face)

> Ok I'll take a swing! Get your plate ready... dish being served.
>
> So you ladies know I joined that virtual dating site. Zero percent chance of being catfished right? Yeah well... I met Tock. True eye candy! Ladies let me tell you; the man was very well spoken, and looking at his place in the background... I was sprung! But girl he had a dog! In the kitchen while he cooking. Oh and he call himself showing me could cook. Aint washed hands the first. I'm like uuuug this nasty... uuug
>
> I aint gone be wit no nasty motha flubba. I blocked em. Rather be alone than with a ratchet Robert.

(She rolls her eyes up in her head and snaps.)

CAMMI:

> What you need to do is stay off them dating sites. If a man aint got no conversation in person... he must have some social issues. Either that or there's something to hide. He was probably doing that cooking demonstration, while his wife was out of town on her girlfriend trip. He's probably always cooking, because he aint never working.

He does ALL the cooking, because she pays ALL the bills.

What you need to do is... date one of the brothers from the church.

Let's hear from you Miss Tish! Come on... give us the dish.

    TISH:

No momma Cammie. I'm still letting what Rita was regurgitating finish resonating in my skull. Not to mention your take on the whole virtual encounter at the kitchen counter with the dog an all. I organized the call. Yawl go 1st

Come on Momma Cammie... let's hear your dirt

    CAMMI:

So I'm in the store last night, getting some wine and cheese to go with my late night poetry. I can feel some eyes burning a hole in my jeans as I'm looking at the wine. My booty cheeks were actually hot! **(they all start laughing)** I can hear the footsteps behind me as I pick up my cheese and make my way to the check out.

Believe it or not... as bold as you 2 know I am... I was scared to look back and see who it was. I decided to fantasize about how fine he was. In my mind his hair had just hints of grey, he was about 6 feet, with a muscular stature... not too bulky though; his hands were BIG, and his feet were huge! He was wearing really nice shoes, dark blue slacks, and periwinkle blue collared shirt with cufflinks.

Yeah ... I know. I'm at Trader Joe's. Whatever! This is my damn fantasy. (they all laugh)

Anyway, curiosity killed the cat. I turned around just as my secret crush was saying "Hey Beautiful".

I looked with both shock and disappointment and said, "Heeeey Sistah, thank you for the compliment". Then I speed walked to the register! (They all laugh) Yep I felt some type of way! Mostly scared though. (she laughs)

Ok now Tish... yo dish!

        TISH:

Ok so... Rick decides it's ok to have lunch dates with female classmates from this new drama class he's taking.

        RITA:

I'm sorry ... What?!

        CAMMIE:

Where they do that at? And drama class... Chick What?!

        TISH:

Right! So I'm like, "Bae, I'm not really cool with that." He tells me how that shows a lack of support and pettiness on my part. Then he needs some air to clear his head. So I tell him... "Yep, that's cool Bae. Sometimes a walk is good to reflect on previous speech. I'll be reflecting on the opposite side of the street." We in this together. That is unless you want an advance class in drama, right here at home!

RITA:

Why are you still wasting time with that fool?! What you need to do is drop him; because you're worth more. I wouldn't take half the mess you've taken off of him. What you need to do is move on.

CAMMIE:

For real though sis! Give up the dream. Take your power back. You're so creative and beautiful. What you need to do is go to the jam session and see what's up with some of them artsy types. You always goin through wit him. Why are you holding onto that man?

TISH:

Because I like having a man; instead of a vibrator or rolled up sweat sock! I aint tryin to be bitter and home alone... sleepless in seattle

Thanks for listening hens! Time for the rest of my day to begin... BYE

(Conference disconnects abruptly)

(Narrator turns to the camera and speaks to the audience)
NARRATOR:

Now see all that could've been avoided if Tish had kept her business to herself. Married women or women who are booed up, should never share bedroom issues, relationship problems, etc.; with their single friends. These women are obviously not relationship experts; they are after all, single.

THIS PAGE IS UNAPOLOGETICALLY BLANK

DAILY SKITz

DINNER WITH RICK'S MOM

NARRATOR:

Hey friends, this skit begins with Tish, Cammie, and Rita at the bar. The 3 are talking about the dinner Tish had to endure with Rick's mother; and how gross the food was.

Tish is currently in a relationship with her boo... Rick. Occasionally Tish will organize mini conferences with her besties to vent about whatever issue she is having with Rick. In essence... letting her girls in on all the business. Now Tish doesn't care how or what is going on in their lives. It's usually nothing anyhow. They are single and getting little to no action. Here's the latest dish or tea if you will.

TISH:

(Walking into the bar with a scowl and clearly a story... She greets the besties in a way only Tish can)
> Gurlz! I need the big glass today. No wait... just have the bar tender put a straw in the wine bottle! This day... this day aint happening. I refuse to believe this is any more than a nightmare. Somebody wake me up!

RITA:

(Calls the bar tender as she shows concern for her girl)
> AWWW! HONTY! What has he done now?

CAMMIE:

(Looking at Rita in disgust)
> Now see why do you always have to assume it's a man thing?

I got 99 problems... He aint even in the mix! Hell I aint even met him... and yet Rita... I still have problems

TISH:

(Places her straw in her bottle of chardonnay)

Ok now look; every man, if he is about anything, got a soft spot for mommy. It's one of the things I love most about my man.

But if your momma's smothered chicken, is looking like something that is evolving into a bubbling alien... respect or not... I aint eating it.

Now if she asks me why... why am I wrong for being honest?

RITA:

Okay, taking back my initial question. Posing another...

Girl what did you do?!

CAMMIE:

Better yet heffa... what did you say?!

TISH:

(They all laugh and sip)

Anyway....
She looked at me and asked...

What's wrong with you? You too good for smothered chicken? What yuppies don't like soul food?

RITA:

This woman did not fix her lips to call you a yuppie.

CAMMIE:

To damned close to puppy if you ask me?!

CAMMIE:

So what was your response Miss Tish?! I know you got her told.

TISH:

Right! So I'm like, "Mam, I love smothered chicken. My granny cooked it with homemade biscuits. I didn't know this was smothered chicken. I couldn't tell what it was. I didn't recognize the smell either. Now that I know what it is ... I have to be honest... I am even more hesitant to eat it. Must be the yuppie in me. My food has to look and smell good to me. Otherwise I just can't.

RITA:

Girl! I'm scared to hear the rest of this story.

CAMMIE:

Keep it 100 sis! Pure comedy... but 100 though! What did Rick do? What did pretty Ricky say?

TISH:

This man's face contorted like you have never seen a face contort. He said, "Hey! That's my momma!" So I said, "Hey! I'm your woman! Which is something you seem to forget when we get around your family. Your momma asked a

12

question and I answered in the same energy the question was posed.

On that note... It is obvious that I have worn out the welcome that I never received anyway. Good luck with that chicken.

Rick, I'm taking MY car, you can get a ride from your mommy.

RITA:

Girl! What does that mean? Are you good? Did you all break up?

CAMMIE:

Chick is it safe for you to go home? You done left this man at his momma's after cursing moms out at the fam dinner... You need my sofa tonight or what?

TISH:

Oh he yelled and screamed to the top of his lungs about how I betta know that blood is thicker than water. He gone hold his family down. He don't go against the grain. Then after I got in the car... here come the text a thon!

Babe... you know my momma be trippin. You like the only woman I ever brought to the family dinners. She just J babe. I'll be waiting up for you when you get home. We gone watch our favorite movie... Which way is up.

Then a few minutes later he was calling. I sent him to voicemail.

I can't melt Rick and pour him out of my life. He aint going nowhere... just like I aint eating his momma's smothered or murdered chicken.

(They all laugh and drink more wine)
(Narrator turns to the camera and speaks to the audience)
NARRATOR:

Tune in next time to see another tale of Tish.

DAILY SKITz

SHOPPING ADVICE

          TISH:

(on the mobile phone with Muriel)
> I think I'm gonna logon to Amazon and order an ironing board. Tired of ironing on my kitchen table with a towel.

          MURIEL:

(in the car on the way home, on the mobile phone with Tish, Muriel's sister Renee is also inside of the vehicle)
> Amazon?! Girl No!!! I read on Facebook that Amazon been dealin some shadiness
>
> Order from Ikea!

          RENEE:

Girl neva! Don't you or ya friend eva ...

I seent a video on IG showin racism behaviors from the sales people at Ikea

She need to go to Walmart.

          TISH:

Last week yawl was pulling some ole boycott mess – talkin bout Walmart and the Union... some ole mess

(Tish turns to the camera and speaks to the audience)
> Look... Folks be on some ...
>
> > don't walk on the left side of the street, that's bad jou jou

Don't walk on the right side of the street, you'll be broke the rest of your life

Don't run ... you too big, might cause an earthquake

Don't stand in one spot too long, might be takin up space somebody else needs

Yawl will drive somebody crazy!

It's an ironing board!!!

    NARRATOR:

EVERYBODY thinks they know what's best!

Every consumer has had a bad shopping experience... somewhere.

They can tell you where you should shop.

Guaranteed; What they won't do go to the store of their choosing, and buy you a damn ironing board. Nine times out of ten, they won't even offer you *a ride* to that location... or any other store.

Moral of this skit... Do You!

I AINT IN YOUR SHADOW... YOU IN MY LIGHT
By Miz Floes

Discovery:
Ba'Jezhene' is a popular and well established songstress, writer and producer. Sparked by the business sense of her mother and the creative skills of her father, at 38 years of age, she sets her sights on becoming a headliner at the hottest night clubs in the Emerald City!
Life hasn't been easy for Ba'Jezhene'. For many years she's struggled with people pleasing. She was even more weak, in the presence of or in relationships with men. She seemed to be very attracted to bad risks. For Ba'Jezhene', talented men or at least men who had some type of flare in their skill-set, were taboo. After two failed marriages, three children, and multiple jobs, she'd finally found, what she believed to be... the cream of the crop. Gorgeous and talented, and he didn't seem to be turned off by her three children from previous marriages. In her mind... she'd found her soul mate! After a very short while, the two were married. This family oriented man even legally adopted the youngest two of her three children...what a guy!
However, after the fairytale, the real story began.

ACT ONE
NAIVE

Time: Late Fall, a very dreary, cold, cloudy, wet, rainy day.
Place: Pioneer Square Apartments, Seattle Washington.
Setting: Ba'Jezhene Gets a disturbing phone message
At Rise of Lights:

The sound of the house phone is heard ringing. Ba'Jezhene is outside of her door but can't open it quick enough to answer it. The answering machine beeps and the caller leaves a muffled message. She finally, gets the door opened, leaving her umbrella at the door and stumbles, off balanced though the front door of her kitchenette apartment with three small bags of groceries snuggly, tucked in her arms and she hears the very last few words of the message. Once she puts her bags down, she removes her rain coat; she remembers her umbrella is at the door. She sees her neighbor, Mrs. Waverly and calls out a hello but she gets no reply. Slightly, slamming her door shut, she crops her body with a disapproving pose. shakes her head and sighs. Then sarcastically, makes a snide remark to vent her disdain, saying; "That's why you ain't got no friends now; you old prune. Probably, ain't had a friend since kindergarten; what a hundred years ago?"
She starts to put her groceries away and stops briefly to turn her answering machine on to listen to her messages.

Phone / Voicemail: (voice of Smooth comes from pre-recorded audio or microphone backstage)
Cue Track…

        SMOOTH:

    Hey Baby… it's Smooth. I wanted to talk to you
    before you left the house this morning; but you
    left before I got out of the shower. I got it Baby…
    I got the call yesterday… I got it baby!!!

    I got the shot I've been waiting for… I'm going to
    New York!

BA'JEZHENE':

Wha......(she holds the locket she that holds his picture and has the inscription; " 'til the end of time") she has hanging around her neck.

What the f... YOU going to New York?!

PHONE / VOICEMAIL/ SMOOTH:

I wanted to bring you with me but I decided against it.

Baby we need some space from each other anyway..... and I know you needed to get outta the fog of my shadow.

I know you was tired of being Smooth's wife instead of Ba'Jezhene'... that's gotta be difficult, never getting any accolades for all the work you did helping me to shine; writing lyrics, hooks and arranging the background vocals for my hit record. I want you to know, I really appreciated your help.

But I gotta pursue my dreams and in that I need to be with someone that can nurture and understand when I need to be a man... Nicky and I just gel baby... I know that hurts... but I'd rather you hear it from me... you'd do the same if the tables were turned.

BA'JEZHENE':

This Mutha ... Really?! All the years... this lil yamp!

Wow... you appreciate me?!

This is madness! (sighing and moved to tears)

I forgave infidelity... And still!!!... he with this female!

(Sitting down on the sofa, she looks at the machine)

You said 'til the end of time...

(Frustrated and angry)

Damn... what a difference a day makes!

After everything ... leaving me behind...

I made your ungrateful ass!

Low life!

(Snatching off the Lockett and throwing it to the floor, she lifts the phone and dials)

Hey Girl, what you got going tonight... I could really use some girl time... a shoulder.

Girl I have given this man my all and he just leaves... not even like a man!

He sneaks off with this lil tramp. ---Yes, that one... his old raggedy drugged out baby's momma.

Girl I am fighting mad, and I need my ride or die to come by and help me kill this fifth of Peach Ciroc!

Oh, no Girl... keep your plans... my emergency is not your urgency.

Hit me up tomorrow ... I'm sure I will still need you. I love you too girl... be safe.

She hangs up the phone and walks over to the mantle where there are several pictures of Smooth and her together, she picks up one, stares at it for a few seconds and then briskly walks to the kitchen and gets the trash can, throws that first picture in the can. Feeling relieved, she looks at the rest and then goes back to the mantle and one by one she trashes the rest.

*Cue Track – I Don't Know Why I - Ba'Jezhene' sings I Don't Know Why I

        Ba'jezhene':

Speaking to the audience:
(Wiping the tears with her pinky)
    See, that's what you get when you do all you, can to help a man become all he can be; Suddenly... You become a damn has-been... Shiiii! I'll be the first to admit; I've been had...

but I'll be damn if I'm a 'has- been'. Honty No!!! ... see that would mean that I am; (counting the fingers on her left hand with the pointer finger on her right hand)

(Finger 1) antiquated

(Finger 2) dusty

(Finger 3) musty

(Finger 4) old

(Finger 5... the middle finger) and ... a wanna-be?

Honty Please... take a real good look at me...

(motioning her hands to show off her sexy shape)
    Do I look like I'm antiquated, dusty, musty, or old?
No Honty!!! Not Ba'jezhene'...

Nothing old... nothing dried up

(turning her back to the audience and showing her butt)
    Noooo honty...I got plenty of ass!

Just like Beyoncé, J-Lo and Niecy Nash!!! ...

The Fog of his shadow... what the f... (She mutters to herself)

It's that fool is living in a fog... the fog of that female he keeps chasing...

(She now begins the spoken word piece ... try love)

I was conflicted... thought you were gifted

Thought we could grow

Back then I didn't know

The depth of your ignorance

In my defense

I was blinded by the bright lights

And big city

Ignored times that you showed me gritty

I took pity

When I should have walked away

I made a conscious choice to stay

Not knowing that you'd rather

Go through the chaos and drama

Just for the chance at reuniting with your baby's momma

Yes the she ... that breaks your heart constantly

The she that no longer desires a he

You're so sad... passed up every opportunity you had

To live the life that was intended...

Her ill actions you've constantly defended

All the negative energy expended

Why? I was standing here...

You could've given true love a try!

The babies you made with this woman

Are now full grown

They've got babies of their own!

And still she's on your mind, in your pocket and calling the cell phone

Why? I was right here with open heart and arms ready to give true love a try...

Yet you'd rather say goodbye...

BA'JEZHENE':

I can't be killin no 5th... I got a show tonight. He can't kill my vibe. Nooo Honty! dollars to earn!

(lights dim and come up as the set has changed to night club design and Ba'jezhene' is on stage singing "U Should Know")
V1

Just in case you didn't already know

These feelings I have for you continue to grow

Deeper and deeper

With each passing day

And if you didn't know… you still take my breath away

Chorus:

Baby you should know

Because I tell and show

You that I truly care

Whenever you need

Baby, I'm right there

You were made for me

You enhance my glow

And anywhere you wanna.. I'm gonna go

You should know

V2

Used to … treat me like royalty

Never ignoring me

I couldn't find a better love

In any time or space

I'd tell you these things everyday

But I thought you knew I felt this way

Chorus:

Baby you should know

Because I tell and show

You that I truly care

Whenever you need

Baby, I'm right there

You were made for me

You enhance my glow

And anywhere you wanna.. I'm gonna go

You should know

(track fades… lights dim and come up as the set has changed back to the living room sofa)

BA'JEZHENE':

What's Up heart ache? Thought I'd ridded myself of you long before.

Guess you were just on the other side of the door.

Feelin like a loser in this life…

I pride myself on being a good woman, I have given this man my all. I lost myself inside him. Part of me feels void of direction. Don't know where to go… who I am… Damn

Why can't a sister see a man in a situation and leave him alone… why she gotta move him over to her side of the street

Why can't these lazy ass women find their own men and leave married men with their wives…

Thots, belly tops, and ass shots… that's what's on the menu today

Get your own man tramps! Home wrecking tramps!

Let me calm down and check myself…

What's mine can't be taken, you can't rape the willing

He walked over to that side of the street… she didn't drag his sorry ass!

(track ends lights go to backsplash or just soften… the spoken word dialogue begins and a soft jazz accompaniment will pace the rhythm)

SISTAH'S YAH HEAR ME?
BA'JEZHENE':

(Expressed with deep, emotional feelings)

Sistaaaah's, I…I… just can't say his name; I feel so ashamed…

he left; after all I've done; forgiving him when he was wrong,

mind scrambled and weakened from his carrying on,

you know what I mean…the other women he'd seen

Always holding on;

trying to be that "woman-strong"…

Shiiii…not wanting to be left alone!

even knowing he was lying with every breath,

and even though it hurt to death,

I went along; played music for that sad, sack song.

You know the one...

(sing songy whiny voice) Baby it will never happen again,

(Speak) yep... he used that line every now and then.

The fool? I was not... the lies I never believed

no my sistahs, I wasn't at all deceived;

just wanted to have his love,

What the HELL!!!!, was I thinking of?!!!!!!!

(Sing) SISTAH'S, CAN YAH HEAR ME?

It's not that I can't remember his name

it's the fact that when I use it,

I remember all the pain

(Sing) SISTAH'S, CAN YAH FEEL ME?

(With hands on her hips)
    You know... I had hopes of being happy for the rest of my life

    no longer a single female

but a loyal and devoted wife.

He was supposed to take me with him to a private paradise.

Hell! That didn't happen; he decided to take another, feeling no guilt…

I REFUSE to cry over spilled milk

(Sing) SISTAH'S, CAN YAH HELP ME? sistahs…

(waving her hand in the fashion of goodbye)
Can you help me wave goodbye, good riddins…

(she makes a megaphone with her hands and yells)
Sistahs…Help me tell him and her … so long!

'cause he damn sho' can't come back here… he can no longer call this… his home!

(Ba'Jezhene walks slowly off stage while speaking to herself)
(Lights fade to black and curtain closes)

INTERMISSION
ACT TWO
LOOK AGAIN

Time: 2 years later
Place: Wellington Estates, Bellevue, WA.
Setting: Ba'Jezhene' new look, new style, new attitude is clearly apparent in this act. She has a diary in her hand and is orally speaking the words she is writing.

At Rise of Lights:
Ba'Jezhene is talking the phone (we hear the last of the conversation which she is ending)

BA'JEZHENE':

Dad I'm not ... how can you say that when you aren't even here?!

You're over 3000 miles away and you're telling me how it is ova here.... Honty Please!

Look here... this man aint stopping nothing for me. I have just taken time to better me...

Hold on Dad... someone is on the other line....

Hello... Yes this is she... What date is it that you're trying to book?

Yes Sir Mr. Degere... I do have that date available. Are you looking for a trio or a full band?

I can do that... we will see you then. Looking forward to it! Have a good day.

(she smirks to herself as she clicks back over to her other conversation on the line)

You a trip Dad… I know you called that club owner down there at Che' Amore!

How did he get my number dad? I told you I already have 2 other gigs that day… I know they are short… still I could've contacted them next month and gave myself a little break…Whatever, I didn't take no 2 year break, I did small gigs here and there… OK DAD! … the gig is booked.

Now I gotta go… I need to get these musicians material and make sure they put this performance on their schedules. I love you and I will take some video and send some pics of the Che' Amore gig.

Okay… k… talk to you later

(when the conversation is over, she slowly hangs up the phone, picks up the wine glass on the table where the phone is (it's a land line not a cell phone), and looks into the audience and smirk-smiles. Then she positions herself on the sofa, (a cocktail table sits in front of the couch) with legs prompted up, her wine glass half full, (already in her hand) and the smooth jazz playing in the background, sets the mood and tone of her expressions. She takes two sips (slowly), smirks again and sighs as she raises her eyebrow and then looking over at her appointment book, she thinks to herself (we hear the thoughts because she speaks them aloud):

BA'JEZHENE':

I got to write this shit down!!! 3 gigs in 1 day!

(then she picks up the appointment book, grabs the pen on the cocktail table, and begins to write.)

YEEEESSSS HONTY! YEEEES! (she says as she slams the book back on the table)

SHINE!

(Spoken Word piece begins here)

Hook:

Blinded by the pain

Nearly drove me insane

Life brought me a change

I was lost

Now I'm found

You can't keep a good woman down

Thought you could trump me

Never will you stomp me

I have purpose and worth

I've been relevant since the date of my birth

I'm gonna shine this little light bright

It's my God given right!

I'm taking flight

I am not in your shadow

It does not define me

Aint got time to be

Sorting through the stress of your mess

You no longer possess

Any space in my head

Put that drama to bed

Got big names calling me

Tryin to be

The next sensation

Spanning across generations

Gonna blind you with my light

That's right

On stages all over town

The name to know in Puget Sound

Now I'm published and recorded overseas

Negro please!!!

Your shadow… that's all you see

A shadow of the man you used to be

When you were in the winner's circle

Accompanying me!

No that shadow can't block this light

I've got 3 shows tonight!

Bling, Bling

Hear my telephone ring

Booking shows and time in studios

Brand new clothes

Think I passed

Your sorry ass

In my Maybach last night

That's right… that's that shine bright

That powerful feminine light!

I'm grinding… I'm shining

Yeeeessss Honty!!!

Your shadow's cast… a thing of the past

BYE Smooth!!!

Keep your black ass shadow

Out of my light!

Hook:

Blinded by the pain

Nearly drove me insane

Life brought me a change

I was lost

Now I'm found

You can't keep a good woman down

(as lights dim , she removes her bathrobe to reveal and evening dress and walks out of a door on stage into a night club setting stage right, where there has been a riser set for her to stand and sing the final song!)

***I Don't Know Why I- by Miz Floes

> V1
>
> I could fill a river
>
> With all the tears that I've cried
>
> I feed a village
>
> If I had nickel
>
> For every one of your lies
>
> You left me standing all alone
>
> When I needed you most
>
> I never asked you for that ring
>
> I just wanted to be close
>
> Chorus:
>
> I don't know why I
>
> Can't stop thinking about you
>
> I don't know why I
>
> Feel like I can't make it without you
>
> I don't know why I
>
> Can't seem to break away
>
> I don't know why I
>
> Didn't leave you yesterday

V2

I can't explain it

Not even to myself

Just the sound of your voice

Still makes me melt

I can't find it in my heart

To refuse you anything

Although I know the truth

I stay trapped inside my dreams

Chorus:

I don't know why I

Can't stop thinking about you

I don't know why I

Feel like I can't make it without you

I don't know why I

Can't seem to break away

I don't know why I

Didn't leave you yesterday

Bridge:

At first sound I didn't process the question

Simply uttered an answer

Upon recollection

And examination of the situation

I now realize that he meant we

But this can't be

I work diligently to keep him happy

I struggle to understand

What it must be that's troubling my man

I refuse to crumble

I was hoping I could build with you

Hoping we could grow together

I honestly believed we could make a divine connection even better

Better me... Better you... as good as we were as individuals... we could be a mind blowing experience as two.

(As the music fades... a SLIDESHOW on overhead projector begins and the lights dim, Smooth Sits alone in a corner of a night club mirroring the night club that Ba' Jazhene is singing in... in his hand he holds a single rose, and sips glass of wine with his other hand... looking sad... as if he is defeated without ever fighting.... knowing he has no chance with the woman SHE has realized she is). Track and Slideshow end simultaneously ... End Show

"HE'S MASSA'S BREEDA"
By

Miz Floes

SPOKEN SOUL

Thinking about past lives

Tweaked DNA… altered bloodlines
That was another time
No choice
No voice

Okay
Guilty I be
It was I that shook the poplar tree
searching for my ancestry
here's a tidbit of herstory
because history is often told

NARRATOR

Salutations theater lovers!

Today we present to you…

MASSA'S BREEDA – A SPOKEN WORD THEATER PRESENTATION

This short, yet important story takes place in the brisk fall season; early 1800s

We're on the Thomas Plantation in beautiful Choctaw County Mississippi. Although normal activity; the unthinkable is about to happen for the thousandth time or more. That is to say…. This has happened many times before!

Indeed there is trouble brewing for a young plantation transplant. Menti Hampton was just sold onto the Thomas plantation. Menti is 7 years beyond the age of advancement to womanhood. This simply won't do here on the Thomas plantation. Menti will be offered up to the plantation breeda today.

A few female slaves, Emanaline, Pet, and Hattie are speaking to the fresh implant; the young miss Menti.

The women attempt to give Menti the birds and bees accelerated course, as they coax her to follow them to the breeda's cabin.

Their task is proving to be somewhat difficult. These desperate women will have to do more to ease a tender Miss Menti into the idea of shedding her girlish ways and entering womanhood. How do they ease a girl into the very robbery of her virginity?

As difficult as the task at hand may seem; this isn't the first time this scenario has played out on the Thomas and countless other plantations. Welcome to what slaves around these parts call… the **situation** (*pronounced sitchy ashun*).

FADE IN:

MASSA'S BREEDA

**Full Lights*
The scene opens with Spoken Soul walking across the stage from stage right, humming the hook to her poem. In the background Rosa (dressed as an elder slave woman), is walking onstage with a broom in hand sweeping. At the conclusion of Spoken Soul's lines… Rosa advances to center stage and as she reaches center stage she addresses the audience, with a bow of her head.

SPOKEN SOUL

One upon a time, she had **no choice**

Way back when all ears fell deaf to the sound of her voice

Back when the age of advancement was a mere nine

Back when they did whatever they wanted to the women of **my bloodline**

over 200 years… Black blood, sweat and tears

Predating the Tic Tocker, Instagram Influencer, Facebooker or the Snapchatter

Back before the women's suffrage,
and #Me Too movements
Back when you would have been hung

After they took your tongue

For uttering the words… "Black Lives Matter"

Baby girl would've

surely grown wings and flown away

if she could've

yet she was forced into womanhood

before the definition was even fully understood

This here be …
the story of my 5th great paternal grandmother… Menti
She wasn't allowed to use her Mississippi Choctaw tone
There were many others like her… in her suffrage
she was not alone

ROSA

Welcome to the Thomas plantation yawl! Yes indeed… welcome one and all! This here be the largest plantation in Mississippi's, Choctaw County!

Today be a truly dreadful one. What be causing lil miss Menti her frustration… today be the day of her situation. You see this be the day that a young Miss Menti, is to be deflowered. Po chile… she done gone and got in her head … and now she's all the fright fo it

Indeed… on this very day, Big Jim Gibson gone steal away Miss Menti's most precious treasure. Big Jim… he ain't no slave. Naw… Big Jim be free! See, Big Jim a Choctaw native that Massa Thomas employ as his breeda.

Das right… Big Jim keep the slave population growin here on the Thomas plantation. That be his only duty round here.

Now, young miss Menti ain't native to the Thomas plantation. Naw, she freshly sold here, from the Hampton plantation of White County.

*Full lighting is dimed… with track lights at center stage.

*Prior to the scene opening, instrumental plays while Rosa sweeps and exits stage left. Menti is already positioned center stage (dark til Rosa exits the stage, then spotlight on Menti as she begins to whimper while speaking). On queue Hattie and Pet **run** on stage from stage right.*
 (Whimpering manner)

MENTI

Why Lawd? Why?

Why'd you allow Massa Hampton to sell me off from my Maw and Paw?

Now dat ole breeda gonna take my treasure

While I'm sho it'll be his pleasure

I's don't wanna let it go

Don't want no parts o what lies hind that cabin door (doe)

Can't find no escape from this here… situation

Lawd help me find a way off this here Thomas plantation

Song – Wish I Could Change His Mind

MENTI

Cocoa colored complexion

He says I's shaped like an hour glass

Wants me in the **situation (sitchy ashun)**

Thangs is movin too fast

What am I gonna do?

Mama said save my treasure

Soon it'll be gone... forever

What am I gonna do?

Where am I gonna go?

Can't hide from you

So I guess its oooo ver noooow

End of song

MENTI

(Spoken) Sho wish I could change his mind

(heavy sigh)

HATTIE

Menti! Menti! – Big Jim callin fo you

Come on here chile... I gots my own chillin to tend to!

Gal we's all done experienced the situation *(sitchy ashun)*

Nobody got time for all this here hesitation

PET

Gal I can see you... I knows you hear Hattie calling you

Supper done ... time fo you to get on ober to da cabin

Quit your foolin Menti!

Iffin you don't wants no complications

Get on ober to da cabin and

take care o da situation *(sitchy ashun)*

*Menti tries to run while the other two females block her path
*Pet gets and holds Menti in her grasp

MENTI

Lawd please hep me!!! I knows you can hear my cries

Sho don't wants no trouble

This here be a terrible place… I's jes wanna leave!!!

If in Paw was here wit me… he'd talk to Massa fo me

Dis here mess would be no mo

I's wouldn't hab ta go in dat dere cabin door (doe)

and gib dat nasty ole injun my treasure today

Momma says dis here is mines

til I's decide to gib it way

Don't care nothing bout what them other gals says

HATTIE

Well yo paw ain't here!

Gal every part of yah belongs to Massa Thomas

Hush that foolishness and come on here

We's tasked to deliver yah to da cabin

Quit yo foolin and come on

PET

You betta stay on Massa's good side

Punishin on the Thomas plantation be severe

Hush up now

What all the fuss fo any ways

*Menti flees the grasp of Hattie and runs toward Emanaline who is walking on stage

EMANALINE

What's all this squabbling?

Miss Menti what you all the fright fo?

Pet, Hattie, ain't no chores need tendin?

MENTI

Please help me Emanaline

They wants my treasure

I's got a right to keep it… my momma done told me long ago

PET

Dis gal gone get us all beat.

Emanaline you gotta tame her

She round here talkin bout rights

How it aint right… she gotta right to choose

HATTIE

Rights?! Who gib her those

She aint Riiiight… in the head

Guess das how it be on da Hampton plantation

Here on the Thomas plantation Massa gots de only rights!

2nd Song -YOU GONE BE HIS

HATTIE

Sings:

Menti listen to me chile

I'm begging you please

I's tryin to let you know

jes what Big Jim sees

and why he needs

to be the air you breathe

MENTI

Sings:

You can stop right there

Wit all that you sayin

I's been talkin to my God

Doin a whole lotta prayin

I knows what right

And I knows what's wrong

I ain't a knock a bout

I knows what's goin on

Chorus:

HATTIE & PET

Menti!

HATTIE

Please Listen to Me

MENTI

get yo self away from me

HATTIE & PET

Menti!

HATTIE

Chile you'd betta listen to me…

Aint no lie in the truth of this reality

HATTIE & PET

You gone be his

And that's the way it is

You gone be his

And that's the way it is

End of song

PET

You bes not be makin no trouble fo us gal!

EMANALINE

Oh... all dis huck a buck be bout the situation

Yawl hush all that fuss

Leave dis chile be!

EMANALINE

Look here miss Menti

Dem tears ain't gone do you no just

Chile trust

Few seasons past ... my eyes seen dis here time

Shoot... the very place you standin in... was mine!

HATTIE

We's done all been here shug

Some of us ... more times than others

You aint getting no pass here on the Thomas plantation

No such a thang round dese parts

PET

Awww, Taint all that bad now

Hurt a lil pinch at start

Fo you knows it, you lookin to see him again

HATTIE

Mmmm hmmm. Chiiiiiiile!

PET

MMMPH! … WHEEEEW!

3rd Song It's Gonna Always Be the Same
PET

Menti chile stop this whining

it aint gonna betta

dry them eyes

quit cryin

it's done been like dis forever

it aint gone change

it'll always be the same

jes know you aint to blame

Chorus:

it's a dog on shame

but it's gonna happen again and again

again and again

gonna happen again and again

Song ends here

PET

Menti Listen to me… this here be jes the first time

Now dere he go… calling fo yah

Go on gal hold up yo head

careful not to look him in his eyes

put a smile on your face

hide what you feeling inside

EMANALINE

(Chuckles sarcastically, then looks serious)

Hattie… Pet… now I members a time I had to walk yawl down to the cabin. I's don't remember such bravery on your parts either

I do remember drying a bucket o tears… had to wring my apron dry

Now yawl leave her be!

Miss Menti, I ain't gone says… you gone cherish this here day

Ain't gone tell yah… wit some time dis here gone fade

Menti… sometimes memories last

Sometime the pain… it don't pass

****Full lighting … with track lights*** *at center stage.*

sound systems plays instrumental accompanied by Miz Floes spoken word performance. As she speaks a soul style dancer faces the audience and dances ... as Miz Floes continues to deliver spoken word.

SPOKEN SOUL

(SING)

No No No No

Please... I don't want to

No No No

Please suh.. I beg you

(SPOKEN)

Birthing a baby today just so Massa can sell it off tomorrow

Ain't nobody even got a tear ... she can borrow

Tears been cried round them parts so many times

folks are literally cried out

The wells of their weary tear ducts... bone dry

Yet the anger remains and is ever present

Everybody knows damned well why! ...

He took it from her!

Ain't never gave Big Jim and no other man permission

No family ... there to protect her!

Massa had already planned and executed that division

They's got ta do as Massa say

That's all they heard... every single day

Much to their dismay... they'd also hear the oppressors say that dreadful word... NIGGAH!

DAMN!

I say no matter the skin color

A baby girl should be loved nurtured and raised up right

By her mother... not some other

She was sold away to

Even they were supposed to clothe and feed her

Not send her off to suffer rape at the hands of ...

Massa's Breeda!

Damned that man

Now... She may never understand... love

*Dancer stops, Spoken Soul exits stage left)
*lights down on Stage, Spotlight up on Pet

PET

Massa still sent me off to them fields

When my belly got full

Still! The plow and harrow I had to pull

Til the day I's birthed my 1st chile

And advanced into motherhood

Just as I fell in love with her smell

Massa sold my baby gal Edna off... like baked goods

lights down on Stage, Spotlight up on Hattie

HATTIE

I remember… that crippling grief

I yearned for the softness of my baby boy's tiny feet

All I could think of was how much… a young buck

depends on his mother

her instruction and nurturing

How much he truly needs… her

They come and took my baby boy from my arms in the frost of the night

he'd been sold off by day's light

Off in the distance I heard Massa's voice

"well ole boy… looks like next season be a good time to see her…

done delivered 11 times for Massa's Breeda

Spotlight down, Full lights on stage

EMANALINE, PET, HATTIE

speaking in unison
    Sometime the pain… it don't pass

*Dim Lights … with spot at center stage.

4th Song - He's Massa's Breeda
Women stand center stage in a circle around Menti clapping and humming a rhythm as Miz Floes begins to sing with soul dancer and music)

EMANALINE

(*SINGS*)

He's gentle as a lamb

But he's strong as any ox

He can be soft as Massa's cotton

And solid as a rock

HATTIE

(*SPOKEN*)

Chile when he hold ya close. Whew!

(Pet shoves Hattie slightly)

EMANALINE

(*SINGS*)

He's sweet as apple pie from my mammie's oven

And even sweeter still, when he's getting the lovin

PET

(*SPOKEN*)

No truer story done ebber been told!

(Hattie giggles slightly)

EMANALINE

(*SINGS*)

He's Massa's Breeda

Big Jim Gibson be his name

He's Massa's Breeda

Don't do you no good to complain

He's Massa's Breeda

All he ebber do is Breed

He's Massa's Breeda

Half dees chillin round here be his seed

He's Massa's Breeda

Chile how you thank I's know

That's Massa's Breeda

He done dis here,

Many, many, many, many… times before

Music fades, full lights, Emanaline takes Menti's face in her hands in a reassuring manner

EMANALINE

Don't fret non miss Menti. Be over fo yah knows it done started. Best thang fo you to do… pray through it.

Pray chile and ask that God take yo mind elsewhere.

What ebba you do… don't fight Big Jim

Jes makes matters worse… then you get beat and you still gots ta do it

HATTIE

I survive to tell yah that there story is true! Now I looks back on it… I made it worse than it was. Now I's long for the nights Big Jim come a knockin… Iffin he don't knock, I's peckin at his cabin door.

PET

Now you look here gal…

If that there don't do you no convincing

We's gone whip ya good if n you gets up whipped

Now you get on in that cabin chile… GET!

Menti exits stage left (into the cabin door), lights down as other characters exit stage left.
Spot Light up on soul dancer and spoken soul

SPOKEN SOUL

So many like Menti

Never even heard a kind word from menfolk

she resented everything about the breeda

getting weaker... her stomach churned with every stroke

No place to run... she couldn't hide

The walls of this here cabin were strong... but they didn't muffle her cries

No No No... Please... I don't want to

No No No... Please suh.. I beg you

Big Jim on top without a care

As Menti lye staring down at her own belly

Wondering what it will look like with a baby in there

Have mercy she thought... when will the pain cease

When will those deaf ears outside ... finally hear my cries

When will I see that cabin door... from the other side

You see... Once upon a time **she**... was regarded as property

Nowadays she's purchasing property!

Thankful **she** is for today

When no means no, women's rights are recognized

She is voting, **she** has the right to wed,

Makes her own choices

takes whomever **she** wants to bed

Damn Massa and his breeda

for the dreadful memories

for the watering down of her bloodline

truly a heinous crime... the deflowering of any girl at the age of nine

Damn Massa and that breeda

for taking what was rightfully hers

in that unholy trans-Atlantic time!

Dancer dances and exits stage left as jazz instrumental is fades in the background and lights go down.
Full lights on stage as Rosa sweeps her way back onto the set stage right.

ROSA

(stops sweeping, looks up at the sky shaking her head, wiping the tears from her eyes with her apron)

*backstage / overhead – pre-recorded sounds of Big Jim and Menti
Umph, umph, umph. Indeed... a sad and yet typical day here on the Thomas plantation.

Mmmmmmm Hmmmm x 3 ... (she hums)

(she sings) Go down Moses, way down to Egypt land... Tell that pharaoh... to let my people go!

Lights down as Rosa exits stage left.
Full lights as soul dancer enters dancing from stage right and narrator's voice is heard overhead, other cast members enter stage right
Miz Floes enters on queue

NARRATOR

Some say the truth hurts.

Ours... is painful history that should never be hidden.

The souls that were sacrificed in our struggle for equality should never be forgotten.

We are sharing this story because we feel knowledge is a powerful tool!

Let's use this tool to teach the future masses about CHOICE.

They say history often repeats itself...

Here in present day...

they've made the decision to overturn... Roe vs. Wade!

The actions of our oppressors should never be repeated!

People use your voice! State your choice!

Before it's too late.

MIZ FLOES

Ladies and Gentlemen thank you for your time and support.

I am the writer and director ... Miz Floes!

In this production I honor my grandmothers both Paternal and Maternal. I honor them by both using their names as well as my voice.

It has been my pleasure to present to you ... **Massa's Breeda**... presented by the Jazzy Sol Theater.

Please offer your applause to this amazing cast of powerful Black women, (introduce cast) and this amazing group of musicians.

CURTAINS

THIS PAGE IS UNAPOLOGETICALLY BLANK

ROYALTY REVISITED

A SOULFUL EXPRESSION THEATER PRODUCTION

MIZ PORTIONTE` FLOES

ACT 1 – GRIOT TIME

DIRECTION / SETTING: *Stage is designed with a stoop and a window. Two middle aged African American women sit on the steps of a building. Just at the entrance; sipping coffee and taking in the scenery of their ever changing community.*

MS BARBARA:

Mornin Lady. Welcome to another opportunity to…
get it right!

MS ROSA LEE:

Grand Rising woman! I got in gear a lil early today; went ova to Brock's Café … got us a couple cups o Joe.

MS BARBARA:

Oooh Yes! Aint you just the sweetest… I couldn't ask for a better neighbor Rosa Lee

MS ROSA LEE:

Sure you could… now you probably couldn't FIND one! And that's to be expected; seeing as how we've be neighbors over 40 years!

DIRECTION / SETTING: *Both women chuckle and sip their coffee.*

MS BARBARA:

Since the 1st grade!
I was just sitting here when you walked up… looking at the block. Then I started remembering all the families that moved away.

MS ROSA LEE:

    I know…. It kind of makes you sad. It actually goes beyond the block; and it's decline. For years now, we've been witnessing the decline of our community.

MS BARBARA:

    Preach! It hurts my heart! The decline of my people's mindsets! They've forgotten their royalty status.

MS ROSA LEE:

    Mainly due to lack of knowledge! Many of these babies don't even know the history of the city… so it stands to reason; they don't know much about the history of our race either.

MS BARBARA:

    I remember my grandfather sitting all the neighborhood children down for story time.

MS ROSA LEE:

    Yes! He sure did! He called it Griot Time. I never knew what that man was talking about. Barbara… what is in the world is griot?

MS BARBARA:

    (chuckles) a griot tells stories about the past, and passes down memories from generation to generation. So when Papa Frenchy would say, "Come on ova here and catch your breath now! You children need some culture." That meant let me give you youngsters some history!

MS ROSA LEE:

He'd say, "All this ripping and running up and down this here block. Set down for a tick. You aint gone grow up foolish on my watch! Sit down here and learn something. Folks had to go through a lot… so you could have the freedom to run and play."

DIRECTION / SETTING: *Both women chuckle and sip their coffee.*

MS ROSA LEE:

Your grandfather was strict! That man did not mix his words.

MS BARBARA:

Who you tellin? Better jump to it… I mean the minute he told you to.
I miss that man; and all the other elders who raised us up in this community.

MS ROSA LEE:

Girl what was the magic they possessed? These kids today look at you like you are out of your mind if you try to give em instruction

MS BARBARA:

Or pull their gun on you, tell you to find you some business. It aint that the seniors back then possessed any magic. Times were different then. Children were different then.

MS ROSA LEE:

It's so discouraging and getting scary too; the drugs, the shootings.

MS BARBARA:

Can't even sit out here and catch air at night anymore. Miss Hazel was burglarized.

MS ROSA LEE:

That poor woman. She's on a fixed income. She aint got nothing for nobody to take.

MS BARBARA:

Honey they stole the meat out of her freezer, her Smart TV, and her tablet.

MS ROSA LEE:

We should do a Go Fund Me or something for her.

MS BARBARA:

I remember when the church would've taken up a collection, or neighbors would've delivered groceries. What is happening to our community?

MS ROSA LEE:

Decline on a large scale Barbara.

MS BARBARA:

I took her a hot plate of food last night. Guess I'll go get her some grocery today.

MS ROSA LEE:

Well I'll have one of my grandkids do a Go Fund Me and post it on their social media pages.

MS BARBARA:

> Well lady, I'm gonna get it in gear and start this day. As always I enjoy starting my day with you.
> You going inside or you gonna soak up a lil more morning sunshine?

MS ROSA LEE:

> Naw... I've had enough morning sun. I'm going inside too.

AUDIO CUE / LIGHTING CUE:

Loud sirens and sounds of gunfire exchange. Screams fill the air. Red and Blue flashing lights should be the lighting effect.

DIRECTION:

Two middle aged women turn to make their way up the steps as quickly as possible and inside the building.

AUDIO CUE / LIGHTING CUE:

Lights down on stage and loud sirens and sounds of gunfire exchange cease.

ACT 2 – THE YOUNG BECOME THE OLD

AUDIO CUE:
Audio track of City Noise (busy streets, cars, etc) plus radio news broadcast reporting the
story of the shooting / police chase from the previous scene

DIRECTION:
The two women from the previous scene are peeking from behind curtains
in their apartment windows one above the other; as the conversation begins
***prop placement TBD**

MS BARBARA: *(peeking out of her window from behind her curtain, she whispers loudly)*
Rose! Rosa Lee!

MS ROSA LEE: *(peeking out of her window from behind her curtain, she whispers loudly)*
Woman! Don't be saying my name! We don't know if they caught them fools that was shooting earlier.

MS BARBARA: Girl I just heard them say on the radio, the suspects were apprehended.

MS ROSA LEE: What?! Well what was it all about anyway?

DIRECTION:
A young woman is walking up the block (the stage) in a hurried fashion, Two other young women are close behind. It's an obvious situation developing. This interrupts the conversation between the two women in
the window.

SHAWN: She need to know who's hood this is! She be in these streets like she earned her place in this hood.

KRIS: Sometimes folks need life lessons. Acting like they read the book and don't even know the story.

JENAÉ : Do you know the story? If you had read my book, you'd know that I am a mother, who pays for childcare. My hurry is in regards to my child and my money. If you read the book of me... in its entirety you'd know that I put my hood on the shelf, years ago... but I can still throw these things. Don't' get it twisted young ones. I'm not your age... I simply look good for mine.

MS ROSA LEE: Young sisters please. It's upsetting to see you at one another like this. We're a community. This is where we lay our heads at night. You can't sleep without peace.

SHAWN : Here we go... Harriet Tubman always got something to say.

KRIS : Girl that's my granny friend, don't be disrespecting her.

SHAWN : Sorry Miss Rosa Lee. She gotta pay her dues to the block though. She disrespectful with it.

MS BARBARA : Is that Shawn down there?

SHAWN : Yes Mam.

JENAÉ : Oh now she got manners... Mam

SHAWN :	You don't want this smoke newbie.
MS BARBARA :	Shawn, stop all that foolishness. That is an adult. She's no teenager. Don't have me call your uncle Sonny; tell him you over here on this block gang banging. This someone's mother you are out here disrespecting. Miss Jenaé she just thought you were her age is all.
JENAÉ :	I appreciate you Ms Barbara.
MS ROSA LEE:	**(with her head hanging from a second floor window)** Alright so now that we have a few more facts. Why don't we take it down a notch, young ladies. You shouldn't disrespect anyone in your neighborhood. This is our community!
SHAWN:	Ms Rosa Lee you didn't hear the way she as talking to us on the bus before we got to the block
KRIS:	**(in a sassy manner)** I apologize for disrespecting your block. I take mad pride in my hood though. I'm doing constructive things for myself. I'm sure it's hard shopping for a new baby's daddy. Sophisticated lady over here, talking down to us like she on a mountain top and she still riding public transportation with us. While her lil crumb snatcher eats off the taxpayer's hard earned dollar!

JENAÉ : What are you doing t that's so constructive? Selling dope, to your best friend's momma? Having yo' lil workers beat-up yo' uncle's woman cause she owes you for a sack? Yeah, real constructive… destroying your community.
You're pushing poison to your classmates and people you've known your entire life. Constructive, huh?
Aint no shame is using the system to get on my feet. When I become a taxpayer somebody else will be able to reap the benefits of my hard earned dollar!

MS BARBARA: Wow! I know my ancestors didn't go through, to get to, only to find this display of thoughtlessness. Personally, I've seen enough! And because I am the deed holder to the property on which you two ungrateful individuals are tongue battling…I can say with conviction…
(Loud and commanding) Put an end to it right now!

KRIS: Miss Barbara! Correct you are! **(The teenager yells up to the window, as she pulls a knife from her back pocket)** Let's skip the start and the middle and get straight to the end of this Ms. Thang!

SHAWN: Aint nothin to it but to do it! Why you gotta be a coward? Put the knife down! You don't need

	that for her. I'll beat the brakes off this ole wanna be young
JENAÉ :	Try it ... them sirens from last night will be back! I don't play with children.
MS ROSA LEE:	**(has come down from her window to join the action , steps in and grabs the knife as she pushes all parties apart)** What's wrong with you two? Have you lost your minds?! Haven't we as a people suffered enough beatings? **(turning to Shawn)** Girl, we suffer beatings on a daily right here in this community. You think they can't pave our roads? You think it aint enough money in the city budget to fix the swing sets in that park? Huh? They've been broken for the better part of 3 years now. **(turning to Kris)** Don't you feel that we as a gender fought hard enough for our integrity? You'd better spend some more time educating yourself on the history of Women's Suffrage, and more importantly, the struggle of the Black Woman!
MS BARBARA:	**(has joined the action on the sidewalk looking at all involved)** Don't you know there's royalty in your blood? Sit down here with me! Ladies, your life has purpose and meaning. It's so much bigger than all this pettiness you're displaying here today. This is small in comparison to the struggles that lie ahead. **(she turns to Shawn)** She is not your enemy, even when she's angry and pretends to be. She is not to be feared, she's not a stranger. She's kin to you and me.

(She Jenaé) She is not to be hated, she is to be educated.

You are all royalty! You should all be respected; you belong to a class that should be protected.
Your community deserves your loyalty... deserves your unity!
Ladies it is together, that we as Blaque Kweenes must run this race. Can't you see that to degrade and belittle her is sheer and utter disgrace?

Neither of you should ever judge a book by its cover.
Every woman in your life today, and every woman that gave birth to her, you, **(she turns to Shawn), (She turns to Kris),** you, and me; We're descendants of and Blaque Kweenes ourselves!

DIRECTION / AUDIO CUE:
Spotlight focuses on Ms Barbara as she begins to sing
Knowledge Is Supremacy

MS BARBARA:

Verse 1
You've been wasting time
When you should have been growing

Why would you choose to live in ignorance
When you could be in the knowing

Knowing that life is what you make it
Please be careful not to waste it
You're close enough to taste it

Chase your fear down then face it

Dare to dream
My beautiful Blaque Kweenes

Chorus

Time is precious ladies
Use it wisely please
Lift your head to the sky
You are of royalty

Take pride in who you are
Be confident and dare to dream
Keep reaching for the sky
You're a beautiful Blaque Kweene

Verse 2
We've come through tough times
The battles have been rough

Fought wars of race and gender
When will you understand enough is enough!

when your sister frowns
whenever she is down
Place your sister on higher ground
Let her know you'll always be around

Know that you are royalty
A beautiful Blaque Kweene

Chorus

Time is precious ladies
Use it wisely please
Lift your head to the sky
You are of royalty

Take pride in who you are
Be confident and dare to dream
Keep reaching for the sky
You're a beautiful Blaque Kweene

Verse 3

You have an image to uphold
Show your ancestors style and grace

They didn't fight through the trenches of time
For you to slap them in the face
Many Kweenes before your time
Were treated so unkind
Still they found the strength to
Do things that would've blown your mind

They had dreams
They were beautiful strong Blaque Kweenes

DIRECTION / LIGHTING CUE:
Spotlight shifts opposite Ms Barbara's position on the stage to Ms Rosa Lee's
position as she concludes the song in the form of poetic verse.

MS ROSA LEE

The Kweenes of yesterday
Struggled hard to pave your way

Their power, smarts and dedication
Afforded you the luxuries enjoyed today

For every note sang on your behalf
You should be appreciative

You didn't always have your say
Some gave their lives so you could live

You are the mothers of today, tomorrow
And the years we've not yet seen
The time to unite is among us
Stand firm as true Blaque Kweenes

Know that you are royalty
Beautiful Blaque Kweenes

SETTING / STAGE DIRECTIONS: Lights dim, Curtain Closes, Scene #1 ends.
ACT 3 – NOTHING AND NOONE GOES UNCHANGED

SETTING / STAGE DIRECTIONS:
Curtain opens and Scene #2 begins.
Blue spotlight focuses on Ms Barbara and Ms Rosa Lee as even older women. They are standing in front of the steps watching the happenings on the block… almost like a time capsule … there is jazz music playing, (an instrumental of EVERYTHING MUST CHANGE).

MS ROSA:

> Yesterday, I saw a brown toned lady, pushing a cart filled with newspaper and plastic grocery store bags. That dirty and grimy, old brown toned lady was **(pause)** Talking to herself like she was half crazy…

Kweene
Bag Lady:

(Shouting angrily w/ slurred speech) Yeah, I know I'm stankin, done been drankin too! If they stole yo' ancestors away from their home land, what would you do? Don't pity me, I do jes swell! Won't be long fo I have eternal piece... and yo' kind, still be here catchin hell!

MS BARBARA:

That dirty grimy lady, shouting and screaming at others;
walking around wrapped in smelly old covers...
She is the descendant of a Blaque Kweene!

Kweene Bag Lady:

I've been robbed of my crown, spat on and beat to the ground.
Still strong as any ox, more clever than any fox
enduring all pain, I will once again reign
I'll use any means, cause I'm a **true** Kweene

MS BARBARA:

Unaware that she's always been in control of her destiny,
Overwhelmed by her trials, she ran scared, never dared, and eventually declared herself unfit for society, she no longer wanted to try to be, she was unwilling to construct a strategy!

Kweene Bag Lady:

(Shouting angrily w/ slurred speech)
"You don't know my struggles,
life aint been no friend to me, don't you dare judge me"!

Can you hear me out there?
Do you even really care?

I'll use my inner mic to be heard
I feel it's important to spread the word
From the junkie to the store owner and over to the nerd
To keep the knowledge to myself would be absurd

You're not listening for the tone of my voice
You're ears are eager to hear my words of choice

My words are never intended to irritate
More so to educate
And also to illustrate

Illustrate the ills of the world today
Illustrating the social injustices, chaos, and natural disasters that cause dismay

Can you hear me out there?
Do you even care?

I'll use my inner mic to be heard
I feel it's important to spread the word
From the junkie to the store owner and over to the nerd
To keep the knowledge to myself would be absurd

A hurricane came and soaked the land, and washed away homes, businesses, and more importantly, lives!
Just before that the Tsunami claimed record numbers, and of those left behind, now some

are selling their young ones, they say it's a means to survive!

Now the water is diseased and famine has stricken the land,
Now many are needed, who'll put their criticism aside and dare to lend a hand!

Can You hear me out there?
Has anyone noticed that the time has arrived?
Is there anyone out there that cares?

I'll use my inner mic to be heard
I feel it's important to spread the word
From the junkie to the store owner and over to the nerd
To keep the knowledge to myself would be absurd

There's so much more to worry about today
People can't we find a way
To help and not be critical
To educate and not to ridicule
Not to reject, but to understand
Your fellow man
If you see I need direction give me a nudge
I implore you, do not judge!

(In a drunken slurred manner / scratching an arm)
Hey. Hey! Can You hear me out there?
Has anyone noticed that the time has arrived?
Is there anyone out there that cares?
(spoken as she exits, stage left)
Awe, shut up! What chu know bout it? You don't care. Quit faking

DIRECTION / LIGHTING CUE:
Lights dim, then lights come up as Kweene Caramel enters the stage scratching her arms and sniffing, approaching a man walking looking pass as if he's looking for something or someone.

MS ROSA LEE:

>I got brave... I was standing out here late last night; got so sad I actually cried.
>Well... tears formed in the well of my... right eye.
>A caramel she, glided directly in front of me.
>There was a man standing on the opposite side of the street.
>He said to her, "What's up love? How you doing this evening"?

Kweene Caramel:

>(sultry tones w/ undertow of intoxication and anxious behavior)

>Ooooh! Hey baby, I'm cool. How about you? You doing alright, tonight?

MS ROSA LEE:

>**He said,** "I'm a little lonely. Wishing I had a friend to spend some time with"?

Kweene Caramel:

>You looking for a girl big daddy or maybe trans is your flavor, boys in drag? Let's play tag?
>I got all you need right here daddy!
>I'm all yours tonight, but spot me ten up front, so I can get this dime bag!

I'll make it worth your while daddy.

MS BARBARA:

I'm surprised last night was the first you've seen her. Kweene Caramel. She represents the schemer, the
Neighborhood's oldest prostitute crack fiend. She's been knocked down, for crack... she's sold her crown! Still considers herself a Blaque Kweene!

MS ROSA:

Our ancestors crossed the waters together
Momma never mentioned days like this
She didn't know of such a life or lack
After all... she lived as a Blaque Kweene in sheer bliss!

Kweene Caramel:

You spend far too much time
    Pointing your fingers at me
    If you knew half of what I been through
    If you only knew the troubles I see
    You don't even know the hell my life has been
    Since I first came to this earth
    I bet you didn't know my daddy left my momma's side
    Eight months before my birth
    You don't know

So don't you dare judge the things I do
You don't know
The trials and the tribulations I'm going through
Always calling me nasty
Talkin bout I don't care nothing for myself
If you fell would it be with grace
Better take a closer look at yourself
You don't wear my shoes
I walk inside them every single day
You talkin what you know nothing about
For your actions you'll have hell to pay!

DIRECTION:

Kweene Redbone enters the stage pushing a stroller with a screaming baby passing Ms Barbara and Ms Rosa Lee.

MS BARBARA:

That poor young soul... Judgmental focus consistently falls upon her shoulders
Whenever she passes by pushing her screaming baby boy down the street in tattered stroller.
Her nerves frazzled, and there's no baby daddy present to console her.

MS ROSA LEE:

That's a shame, she should've been somewhere with her head in a book instead of some little boy's lap.
That's the reason our little black girls can't get no where now!
So busy running up behind these little pissy tail boys.

Kweene Redbone:

(*Sassy tone w/ attitude*)
Don't be pointing yo' finger at me cuz I'm a teenager.
I aint the first person on earth to get pregnant as a

teen or out of wed lock! I fell in love and used bad judgment. But I don't regret my bundle of joy. There aint nothin I wouldn't do for my little baby boy!
Did you ever stop to think things might be better for black girls my age, if black women like you acted your age and gave us some guidance?
All these part time mothers, half raising their children.
I'll raise my son with pride and integrity. If he happens to impregnate a young girl, I'll make sure she has guidance, feels loved, and most importantly, knows she has purpose and worth!

LIGHTING CUE:
Lights dim and Blue spotlight focuses on Poetic Narrator.

MS BARBARA:
Many of you know of someone who has or have yourself walked in the same shoes. You've either received or issued advice that would've prevented what some call "teen mother's blues". Don't throw stones, don't judge her, make an earnest effort to understand her, and don't be condescending or mean. Remember she too is of royalty. Yes she's a teen mother and yet, she's still a Blaque Kweene!

PASSERBY:
If you saw a toddler crying would you…
Slap him and push him on the ground

Then why on earth would you…
put a teenaged mother down?

If you saw a preschooler struggling to tie her shoes
Would you laugh at her and call her a clumsy fool?

Of course not !
You know that she's learning one of life's lessons
That isn't taught at the public school

Remember that many lessons are learned
Through trial and error and sometimes we humans tend to make a mess

You'd better help that young mother…God is watching you… God Bless!

SETTING /
STAGE DIRECTIONS:
    Lights dim, Curtain Closes, Scene #4 ends.

SETTING /
STAGE DIRECTIONS:
    Curtain opens, stage is designed with a stoop and a window and Scene #5 begins. Blue spotlight focuses on Poetic Narrator, and lights come up as Kweene Cinnamon is seated at the window looking out sobbing and grimacing in pain.

MS ROSA:
    My gaze fell upon an open window on the corner across the street.
I watched in horrific agony as Cinnamon Skinned Kweene was punched and then stomped by her husband's feet! Then he threw her out!

Kweene Cinnamon:
    (She sings) – When I climb the stairs
    (Then Speaks cautiously) – I pray that as my key turns the lock, I somehow magically change his mood.

I just want a kind word or perhaps a friendly greetin!
I just can't take another one of those bloody beatins.
(she sobs)

MS ROSA:

90% of the time, she's traumatized and emotionally shattered
bruised and too afraid to tell her family she's being battered
Right now the Cinnamon Kweene is blinded, but she should be reminded… that there's royalty in her blood.
Someone please tell her that she's still a Blaque Kweene!

MS BARBARA:

She sportin that shiner that her husband gave her for her birthday! That low down dog did it right before he confiscated her bi-weekly pay! He done sealed his own ill fate; he'll burn for all eternity. Burn he will, for his part played in the torment and torture of this Beautiful Blaque Kweene!

Kweene Cinnamon:

I'm beginning to doubt my love for him
Well he makes me sad, and he's got me feeling grim

How many times can I hear sorry
And look at the bruises all over me
I think I've got it all figured out
This isn't what love is all about

If I was ever wondering
Whether or not this love was true

I'm over it now

Now that my face is black and blue

Tonight when he lies down to sleep
Out that front door I will creep
I won't even make a peep
I pray to Lord his soul to keep

Never again will I have to lie
About what happened to my eye

He won't have to be sorry
And I won't have any bruises on me

I won't be that woman scorned
I'll be that blessed woman, the one who was warned

I'm leaving his ring, cause I no longer want to be his wife

I may be battered, but I still got my life!

SETTING /
STAGE DIRECTIONS:
    Lights dim, Curtain Closes, Scene #5 ends.
SETTING /
STAGE DIRECTIONS:
    Curtain opens and Scene #6 begins.
    Blue spotlight focuses on Poetic Narrator, and lights come up as Kweene Smokey enters the stage speaking.

MS ROSA:

Now this is where things get real sticky and complicated.
    Embraced by some and by some... hated.
    I'm speaking of the Smokey Topaz toned Kweene!

Kweene Smokey:

(spoken with conviction) Yes, I am content with makin love to my own kind! I don't care if you regard me a fool and say I've lost my damned mind! I'm in love, are you people ALL blind?!

MS ROSA:

She walks upright, she a human being. I know it's my own personal opinion...She is strong and defiant, until the bitter end
Her royalty still lying within
A human being, A lesbian Blaque Kweene!

MS ROSA:

The wildflower she is. She's free within her spirit.
    Her voice is commanding! Many stop in their tracks when they hear it.
    She feels like he within. She made a lover of her best friend. She doesn't view her actions as sin, nor a cross to bear. Her sexual preference isn't contagious or any of your business, so why do you even care?!

Kweene Smokey:

I don't care what you think
Even if I was straight you'd be against me cause me skin was pink

Or green or brown, if I went up instead of down

A closed mind will use any reason, the changing of a season

This is a new day, I'm doing things my way, hear what I say!
You call me a freak...
You'd shun me the same, and call me names if I were a computer geek!

You're looking for a reason to stare
So... what do I care?
Why should I give a damn what you think

You probably think everyone in my racial background is a thief
If that's your belief, your way of thinking stinks!

SETTING / STAGE DIRECTIONS:

Blue spotlight focuses on Poetic Narrator, and lights come up as Kweene Umber walks along the path of the community market.

MS BARBARA:

This pretty little umber skinned lady's on her way down to the community market. She takes the journey every Sunday afternoon.
You see she delivers spiritual enrichment to the locals. She reads the words of the gospels while peeking over her bi-focals.

Kweene Umber:

(Spoken in a soft, kind, yet commanding tone)
The Bible says God is Love. I am a child of God. Therefore I am of him, which
I am love. I once was lost, an alien to God. I was unidentified.
Then my Heavenly Father gave me an identity. He claimed me through my bond with Jesus. He named me a child of God...

MS BARBARA:
> She takes the words of the Bible to bed each night. Not a man!
> She earns sufficient pay each month and with it she does the best she can! What she lacks in material worth, she's more than made up for with her love for mankind! She's a saved and sanctified Blaque Kweene!

Kweene Umber:
> Forgive your brother 77 times 7 times a day! Jesus wants it this way.
> Teach the youngsters the right way to go. Ensure their guidance and help them grow!
> Buried talents are a waste of time. Make sure that yours and the lights of any others in your path shine!

Kweene Umber:
> This cold cruel world didn't give me this love
> And I refuse to allow the world to take it away
>
> Times may get rough, my soul may get weary
> I'll count it as a lesson learned and be thankful for everyday
> Spread his word throughout the land
> Lending a helping hand
> I'll love them in spite of the fact that they shun and push me away
> I'll forgive my brother 77 times 7 times a day
>
> I'll turn the other cheek
> It's the Kingdom of Heaven I seek
> I'll ask the Father for guidance every time I speak

Resist temptation, and forever be meek

SETTING /
STAGE DIRECTIONS:
Lights dim, Spotlight focuses on Solo Vocalist as she performs a gospel song – I NEED YOU TO SURVIVE

SETTING /
STAGE DIRECTIONS:
Curtain opens and Scene #8 begins.
Blue spotlight focuses on 6 Kweenes positioned on the right hand side of the stage, and lights come up as Kweene Bag Lady begins to speak.

1 **Kweene**
Bag Lady &
2 **Kweene**
Caramel:

1Thank you, Ms. Sojourner for preachin
　2Thank you Mrs. Ida B Wells Barnett for your strength and endurance with regard to your reports on racism
　1 and all your school teachin

1 **Kweene**
Redbone &
2 **Kweene**
Cinnamon:

1 Thank you Madam C J Walker
　I appreciate your revolutionizing hair care
　2 Ms. Rosa Parks, thanks to you and so many others I can sit anywhere!

1 **Kweene**
Smokey &
2 **Kweene**

Umber:

> **1** Harriet, please allow me to express my gratitude on behalf of all the descendants of those who partook of your navigated walks to freedom.
> **2** Thank you Mrs. McCleod Bethune for the college and the books; and the wish of a special blessing extended to you for taking the time to educated me, so that I could read em

SETTING / STAGE DIRECTIONS:

> Lights dim, Curtain closes. Curtain opens and lights come up as dancers enter the stage area, dancing to the beat of congas, cowbells, and rhythm track.
> <<Dancers perform a total of five minutes.>> As the dancers dance the following poem plays pre-recoded

THROB!

> I wanna go back
> I wanna go back home
> I was captured yesterday
> and sailed to lands far away
>
> Many slaves will sing that song
> and remember trials and tribulations
> the fears from the minutes of being
> captured to being placed inside cages for holding
>
> Tears form in the wells of a little slave girl's eyes
> as memories of torment invade her mind
> memories of countless beatings and slaps to her face
> the mistress spoke a different language
> the child couldn't possibly take heed to the scolding
>
> In what tongue do these strangers speak
> why am I hated and mistreated

Why did they invade my homeland
Why am I referred to as a dumb ape

Are they not aware that I am human
Why have they placed me in chains
Why should any human suffer this torture, toil
and then rape

I've been robbed of my hopes and dreams
With pain my body is wracked
someone tell me why
When I was brought to this strange land
I tended to the fields, and helped the crops to flourish
I kept Massa's mansion immaculate, cooked and served the meals,
and supplied the Massa's heirs with breast milk
to quiet them whenever they'd cry

I haven't seen my momma
since she was traded for the live-stock
back when Massa saw an opportunity
When that old wagon disappeared down the dusty road
sealed was mine and momma's fate

I knew I'd never feel her kiss again
there was so much I wanted to say
 But I couldn't write momma any letters
back then slaves weren't allowed to read or write
Massa forbade slaves to communicate

Momma was far from me now
Stripped of my identity
I didn't know enough about this new land
I couldn't really relate

Another sale today
now even more

will be held in subjugation
whipped and constrained by chains

Now in the years to come
my children's, children's, children
will come to visit my remains

By then this strange land
will be the only home I know
This once barren place
where I helped the cotton fields grow

The thieves I've helped
have caused the watering down of my bloodline

I had no choice in the matters
All females must succumb to Massa's advances inside the big house
The cut off age for advancement to womanhood...
nine

Yes at so tender an age
I was robbed of my precious fruit

Don't cry for me though
In later years, I got him back
upon Massa and all inhabitants of his mansion
I placed a viscous root
I say silent prayers for my baby brother
who'd lay most of the day at Massa's feet

And most of the night
He was served as Massa's little forbidden treat

Now that he's full grown
he'll provide pleasure to the Mistress

forced to commit adultery
time and time again

Inserting his seed into the wombs
of Massa's captives
while his own bloodline continues to wear thin

Now many descendants of these slaves
will identify themselves as African-American
but that identity, that declaration,
it will not be true

African American only makes reference to citizenship
This misconception of mass deception
We must band together to undo

It's because of the thieves of yesterday
That my tribesmen wouldn't hear me
if I constructed a drum
and beat on it until my fingers bled

The only people who could educate me
on what my roots are and what they should mean to me
have been silenced, sold, hung, beaten or burned
until they were dead

After all the trading, the railroads we've constructed
All the cotton fields, diamond mines, rape and torture,
after all the charges we tended

Still we're regarded as outsiders
No social ties inside the community
No welcome mats extended

No place for the descendants to go
This land is the one and only land they know

The land in which they should be free to live
considerably and equal too

There should be no fight for equal rights
The rights have already been earned
Payment is long overdue

Didn't mind being used
it's the misuse that bothers us most

To add injury to insult
we've been publicly abused
then forced to listen to our abusers boast

After all the revolts
The boycotts and marches
The abolishment of slavery
Race riots and "Black Face"

Still refused
Not accepted as equals
The American descendants of
the African souls that were conned, captured, tortured,
then smuggled here in the first damn place!

**SETTING /
STAGE DIRECTIONS:**
    House Lights up, Cast introductions begin at this point.

THIS PAGE IS UNAPOLOGETICALLY BLANK

4 JAZZY SOULZ

By

Miz Floes

4 JAZZY SOULZ

4 JAZZY SOULZ
Is an exploration of the birth of Jazz, and its positive impact on, underserved communities in multiple cities around the world.
Music is universal. This 30 minute production also provides historical facts surrounding music; while highlighting some of its most notable contributors, and notorious locations.
The production is performed in the style of "spoken word" with musical accompaniment.
This production will be narrated by Momma Jazz.

CHARACTERS

MOMMA JAZZ – Nostalgic Narrator

JAZZY SOUL # 1 – SEATTLE IS THE SCENE... where this soul found its jazzy steam
She's here to hip you to... the Black & Tan!
This is where all the greats performed when visiting the evergreen state.
Those sessions at the Black & Tan were the hottest around.
This cocoa skinned Jazzy Soul is gonna tell you about the "Soundz of the Sound"!

JAZZY SOUL # 2 – HARLEM IS THE SCENE... to which this soul clings
Here to tell the story of the renaissance and Harlem's cool sessions of jam.
This chocolate soul wants to take you to Ella's Place, to experience that Jazzy Bluez.

JAZZY SOUL # 3 – THIS IS THE TOWN... where our spicy, black bean soul first heard that jazzy sound
Here to tell the story of the fictional location ... The Jazzy Soul Station.

JAZZY SOUL # 4 – UNIVERSAL IS THE SCENE... where this cinnamon soul dwells. Here to tell the story of another time and space.
SET: 4 souls stand in a cypher, heads bowed, (their feet will swivel allowing each performer to face the audience during their presentation). Off in the distance, (stage left rear, on a stool with spotlight focused whenever speaking) sits Momma Jazz. Queue band as spotlight shines on Momma Jazz.
The band is playing a jazz instrumental).

MOMMA JAZZ:

(Speaking to the audience)

> Do you remember Nina Simone? She was an amazing soul. Nina was an activist as well as vocalist and musician.

Multi-lingual too!

Fierce she was...

and because Of her activism, social consciousness and contributions to music, as well as black excellence ... the 4 Jazzy Soulz present you with this fused rendition of spoken word and Nina's 4 women.

SET: Spotlight down, center stage lights up on 4 souls standing in a cypher, heads bowed, (their feet swivel allowing Jazzy Sol #1 to face the audience) Queue music /band *Instrumental 4 women starts again

JAZZY SOUL 1:

My skin is black,

What do they call me?

They call me Monkey, Coon, and many other names that don't belong to me.

In this world where I stand not amongst the chosen man...

I don't drive a fancy car. I have never experienced the taste of caviar.

Gay Paris... to date I can't afford to travel that far.

Looking in the sky... I realize that I cannot name even one star!

I was raised by a single mother

Me and my younger brother, took the option of staying strong for one another

We were no strangers to welfare or the "public aid"

After all, that's how our rent was paid

I was my mother's housekeeper, master chef, and receptionist too

Truly... it was a pleasure, assisting with those duties of motherhood

Heaven knows I did all that I could

However, present would come and change us all.

Some came to rise and others... to fall

SET: their feet swivel allowing Jazzy Sol #2 to face the audience

        JAZZY SOUL 2:

My skin is yellow

What do they call me?

Bastard child, daddy's maybe, half breed, useless seed

I have purpose and worth.

My mother has told me this, since the date of my birth!

EVERYDAY, I hold on tight to my shine

I bathe in my wealth

I have got it and I keep it together!

I encompass the power to weather obstacles, turmoil and stress

Why would I ever second guess

My Black and Brown pride and determination

Gonna continue the business of bringing about elevation

leaving no room for devastation

I'm ready and excited about the life I've aligned

designed... for success and nothing less

I will be careful... I will not digress

I have potential

truly this ... is essential

This is the hour to empower

Using my joy to devour fears and tears

SET: their feet swivel allowing Jazzy Sol #3 to face the audience

        JAZZY SOUL 3:

My skin is tan,

What do they call me?

What do I care? They don't ever call me anything nice!

They see me on the stroll selling my preciousness for a dime bag

They call me a schemer, a streetwalker, T.H.O.T, tramp, home wrecking fiend

On occasion, their husbands and lovers call me...

"sweet thing"

And though I may be confused and misguided... there is still royalty in my veins

I call myself a Black Queen!

I mean... just because I fell down, doesn't mean I can't rise again

I can stand... Aint I a woman?

SET: their feet swivel allowing Jazzy Sol #4 to face the audience

           JAZZY SOUL 4:

My skin is brown.

What do they call me?!

I wish they would fix their mouths to call me ANYTHING negative!

They will get the taste slapped directly and immediately from their tongues.

I ... ain't even the one!

What they need to do is use caution, look me in my eyes and realize... they can't whip this thunder!

Time and effort have brought about change

the underground system rearranged

the way the world was once known

still we struggle to set new racial tones!

Didn't have it made

everybody still picking some form of cotton

aint got to be no certain shade

black folks still taking life's lemons

yet we are now conducting seminars on

how to make money selling lemonade!

We came, we saw, and adapted

And we'll keep on striving... we will never stop

Quitters?

NO... we are not

We'll continue to improve and survive

Can't whip this thunder

The day has come to enjoy the Rein!

My name is ... Goddess, Queen, Being Supreme
Black is beautiful... naturally am I

Call me victorious

SET: End music. Lights down on center stage. Jazzy Souls 2-4 exit stage right. Spotlight up on Momma Jazz.
MOMMA JAZZ:

(Speaking to the audience)

What do they call me?

Momma Jazz baby! Ha Ha Ha!

Ok now here is where our story begins my new friends ...

SEATTLE IS THE SCENE where this soul found its jazzy steam

She's here to hip you to... the Black & Tan!

Listen close and stick with her if you can.

The Black and Tan Club located in Chinatown, on 12th and Jackson in the basement of a building whose main floor was occupied by a Japanese-owned drug store.

This Jazzy Soul will talk about this once famous place where all the greats performed when visiting the evergreen state / the Emerald city.

The spot where the sessions could get gritty!

Yet the jams at the Black & Tan were the hottest around.

This cocoa skinned Jazzy Soul is gonna tell you about the "Soundz of the Sound"!

Set: Queue musical track / Queue band for first performer Jazzy Soul #1)

JAZZY SOUL # 1:

I live here...

home of the 12s that break sound barriers

home of the Seahawks and the Mariners

Starbuck's coffee grinds

the constant shuffle of mass feet

as I walk the streets near the pier

I can hear... seagulls singing a song of praise

even hear ferries coasting the waves

feel the breeze brisk on my skin

hear melodic winds

here in the Sound of Puget

I get …

remnants of audio left behind

join me on this musical journey back in time

It was the onset of World War II

Mr. Noodles Smith and Mr. Blackie Williams decided to christen Club Alhambra!

That was the year of 1922

at 404 and a half … 12th ave South

That's the corner of 12th and Jackson

There sat one of Seattle's most hidden, yet major attractions!

By 1932… it was transformed into the Black & Tan

Became home to the Ray Charles Band!

I mean way, way back when Fats Waller made em holler

When it didn't mean a thing without the swing of

Oscar Holden's band

This jazzy bottle club oozed with soundz and featured greats like…

Count Basie, Duke Ellington, and Louis Armstrong

In later years, Charlie Parker, Eubie Banks, Guitar Shorty, Little Willie John, Ernestine Anderson and the Dave Holden band would come along!

Listen... you could hear the vocals of Sarah Vaughn, Ivy Anderson, Etta James, Aretha Franklin, George Benson and Gladys knight too

Put your ear to some Lena Horne, Joe Samples, Stanley Payne, and in 1962... Jimmy Hendrix rolled through

with the Bobby Taylor crew

Soundz of the Sound!

Art and creativity be the emerald city's heart beat

The Sessionz of the Sound are always hot

The Puget Sound has got...

Rap from the Emerald Street Boys, Macklemore and Sir Mix A Lot

Soul blasts from the past

Acapulco Gold, the Septimus, and the Cooking Bag

The great Puget continues to give way to the sounds of today...

We've got Spoken word... if you ain't heard

Ask someone who's experienced and knows

The verse offered by poetess... Miz Floes

In every town around the Sound

There's a jammin session of sweet beats

sounds for him, for her, for them, for you, for me

Soundz of the Sound

Set: music fades, lights down, Jazzy Soul #1 exits stage right. Jazzy Soul 2 enters stage left and walks to downstage center.

MOMMA JAZZ:

(Speaking to the audience)
> Ok now! It is my hope that you caught everything. Because now we're in fuuuullll swing
>
> *and HARLEM IS THE SCENE...* to which this next soul clings
>
> Here to tell the story of the renaissance and Harlem's cool sessions of jam.
>
> This chocolate soul wants to take you to Ella's Place, to experience that Jazzy Bluez.

Set: Queue musical track for first performer Jazzy Soul #2)
– music starts when the performer gets to the line "Baby that joint was jumpin
jazzy bluez was thumpin".

JAZZY SOUL # 2:

> It Don't mean a thing, if it ain't got that swing
>
> Doo Wop, Doo Wop, Doo Wop, Doo Wow
>
> Ah... Good times I am sure Louis can validate
>
> After All he was literally instrumental
>
> in the quest to facilitate Jazz in the city of windy... where he made it trendy
>
> Louis came to town
>
> With that New Orleans sound

He'd come to play

with greats like Miss Blanch Calloway

I'm talking even before the days

When Minnie's Moochin

And low down hoochie coochin

Was on the lips of Mr. Cab Calloway

Yeah Louis set the stage and made many friends along the way.

Like Ella break a glass with her high pitch Fitzgerald.

Yeah times changed quickly though.

The Harlem Renaissance period ended

Some black folks were still singing on stages; some were being burned out of their homes, lynched on back roads, buried in mass graves, shot

Black folks went through a lot!

I kid you not!

The juke joints, bottle clubs, and basement jams were fading fast

Live entertainment ... a thing of the past

If you knew where to look

You'd find that little nook

that feel good getaway

Like... Ella's Place

Now that was the spot

The session was guaranteed to be hot

Baby that joint was jumpin

jazzy bluez was thumpin

out the door and down the block

star studded jam sessionz

that hit the spot

Over and over again

A cool shot of gin

A secret game of craps

Between friends

In the basement of the joint

Made it a point

To keep the noise down

Didn't want the law comin round

This after-hours felt like home

Yet it was upscale and classy

And although Miss Ella could be quite sassy

She knew just how to set a fine and mellow mood

Ella would scat you out your shoes

At the Tuesday night Jam, Bessie Smith would sing the blues

The Divas cleared the way

whenever Lady Day

stopped in

Ella and Billie were **longtime** friends

Two of the heaviest hitting divas of their day…

If you will

Okay… here's the spill

After Harlem's Renaissance, the goodtime spots began to fade away

The world lost great masterful musicians, vivacious vocalists, amazing actors, dazzling dancers

Entertainment… like bad teeth

Started to decay

Now it really aint nobody's business

But at Present… the once incomparable … "Lady Day"

Sits homeless on a crate

Where the doorway of Ella's once stood

And she really ain't lookin too good

Spirited beverages, her only friends

Vodka, Whiskey, Rum, Gin

Whatever she can get

Money she has not

When she isn't beggin in her usual spots

She's resting up inside her cozy cardboard box

Still each day

She makes her way over to say hey

To her good friend Ella,

Who isn't even there!

But you'd swear that Ella was

Because...

the conversations are so interesting

As one sided as they are

Miss Holiday sees herself at that bar

On a stool, legs crossed, cigarette in hand

Chatting with the proprietor Miss Ella Fitzgerald

about, the times of old... When that Jazzy Blues was all up in her soul.

Set: music fades, lights down, Jazzy Soul #2 exits stage right. Jazzy Soul 3 enters stage left and walks to downstage center.
Spotlight up on Momma Jazz

MOMMA JAZZ:

(Speaking to the audience)
    Well alright now! Are you enjoying this eargazm?
    Well now we're headed over to the station.
    Here's the situation

    Time for you to learn about the part of town,
    where our spicy, black bean soul first heard that
    jazzy sound!

    Now enjoy this story of a fictional location ... The
    Jazzy Soul Station.

Set: (Cue musical performer Jazzy Soul #3)

JAZZY SOUL #3:

Don't You Wanna Go?

Don't you wanna ride?

Climb on board

Destination… the Jazzy Soul Station

all aboard this train is moving

to the groove of a brand new rhythm

providing mental stimulation

and energetic elevation

throughout the entire nation

positive and unique beats

inspiring you move your feet

all aboard this funky inspiration

this musical journey

this train is headed to the Jazzy Sol Stay Shun

don't you wanna go

come along for the ride

the funky, neo-soulful and poetic stimulation

melodic and smooth

fused with sentimental grooves

soft rock, R&B and jazz

they've gotta lot of pizzazz

down at the Jazzy Sol Stay Shun

they serve food for the soul

for the rich, the poor, the young, and the old

Don't you wanna go?

I can give you a ride

Just climb on board

Let me take you where jazz resides

Miz is verbally flowing

as the listeners are growing

she's throwing melodic jazzy vocals

off of the stage into the crowd of locals

No joke!

The keyboard player is stroking souls

as his fingers glide across the keys

He funks the crowd out ... melodically

Baba Frenchy takes the beat back to the land of the drum

as he makes his Bongos hum

the sax is singing its own jazzy groove

keepin the beat unique … the drummer gives that foot peddle extra speed

yes indeed… the perfect fuse

don't you wanna go to the Jazzy Sol Stay Shun?

I'm telling you it is the only place where you can get a funky, neo-soulful and poetic type of stimulation

Climb on board

Let me take you where the beats are melodic and smooth

fused with sentimental poetic grooves

soft rock, R&B and jazz

where the band has plenty pizzazz

get your groove on at the Jazzy Sol Stay Shun

Let's go

It's almost time for the show

If we leave now we'll have just enough time to

Hang where the "real" grown folks do their thang

Either ride this train or hit the highway

It's a cool little getaway … especially if you've had a long day

come relax and grow with the soothing sounds

only found at… the Jazzy Sol Stay Shun!

Don't you wanna go?

Don't you wanna ride?

Climb on board

Destination... the jazzy soul station

Set: music fades, lights down, Jazzy Soul #3 exits stage right. Jazzy Soul 4 enters stage left and walks to downstage center.
Spotlight up on Momma Jazz

MOMMA JAZZ:

(Speaking to the audience)
Where did that soul say I could find the Jazzy Soul Station? Because I think I wanna go. I could definitely use a ride.

You know what I mean?

Ever dreamed of touring outer space? What if you could just purchase tickets and go to concerts in other galaxies?

Well get ready for a galactic experience... as this next soul takes us on an expedition to experience the UNIVERSAL SCENE... where this cinnamon soul tells the story of another time and space.

Set: Queue musical performer Jazzy Soul #4)

JAZZY SOUL #4:

In another time and space

I was that bass

Residing inside the beat… so soothing and sweet

I was captivated by the melody

I set free any and all misery

Just gave in

Engulfed myself

A floetic smooth, jazzy connection

Felt like perfection.

My jazzy soul at ease

in the royal purple breeze

Every time Jazz sings to me

I can see the stars

Through the sunshine

Every time the melody holds me close

I let go and elevate my jazzy soul

This jazz thang…

a formulation

For future generations

The development of unique instrumentation, musical molds

The experience is epic

Even universal

Jazz emanated from the hue of the groove's glow

Hence the evolution of my jazzy soul!

Now I don't scat

Because I can't do that

I take a drag of the jazz

And regurgitate verse

Ah yes… that Jazz

It reaches the masses

As it passes… many marvel at what has been heard

The basstastic beats, the melanin fused grooves

The percussionistic fuse

The thump, snap, and fizz

A floetic smooth jazzy connection

Feels like perfection

Jazz has a message that desires to be heard

Every time Jazz sings to me

I can see the stars

Through the sunshine

Every time the melody holds me close

I let go and elevate my jazzy soul

Set: Instrumental solo here as Jazzy Souls 1-3 enter stage left, and Momma Jazz joins the souls as they all reach center stage rear
After all have entered the stage area, solo ends as Jazzy Soul 4 continues …

    I'm captivated, full, and in complete control

    Of my Jazzy Soul!

Set: Full lights

THIS PAGE IS UNAPOLOGETICALLY BLANK

ONCE UPON A JAZZY SOUL

AT THE CAFÉ

Miz Portiontè Floes

ACT 1 – ACTIVE JAZZ

LIGHTING / PROJECTION CUE:
Blue wash for onstage lights plus spot?
Cue slideshow - this silent slideshow with pics of Jazz greats, clubs, and instruments, neighborhoods in Louisiana during the 1920s will run throughout ACT 1, Intermission, and ACT 2

AUDIO CUE:
There is a musical track / impromptu selection playing and tap dancer aka Jazzy Soul Dancer enters stage right. As he reaches the tables he begins wiping, yet he is still dancing (more dancing than wiping)
 *Dancer note: *Careful not to tire yourself out… be real smooth with your movement at some point really get into a groove and forget all about wiping*
After Dancer stops wiping and goes into full on dance
Turn on LAV for Lil Momma Jazz

DIRECTION: *Lil Momma Jazz enters from stage left and begins to voice her irritation with the Jazzy Soul Café dancer – better known as the café greeter / wait staff*

LIL MOMMA JAZZ:

(Speaking to the dancer)

> What are you doing?
>
> Those are not your fans waiting out there.
>
> Chile aint nobody come to see yo lil tail dancing.

Your job here is to clean tables and greet the customers.

You got folks waiting to get in ... while you foolin round out her dancing. Please get these tables wiped down and will you let those ladies in?!

AUDIO CUE:
After Dancer removes stanchion and allows the guests entry
Turn on LAVs for Jazzy Soulz 1-4

JAZZY SOUL #1:

They rioting and ranting out there!

JAZZY SOUL #2:

Right! Flat out in an uproar...

Most folks are afraid to buck the system... so they stick with the program

JAZZY SOUL #1:

Aint enough to lynched and tarred us Even dropped kerosene bombs and burned us out of our homes! Damn shame is what it is.

JAZZY SOUL #3:

Naw the shame came... with what they did to lil Emmit. We as a people should've done more! We have to protect our children.

JAZZY SOUL #2:

I agree. But some folks fight differently. Some protest quietly… with pen and paper.

You Know… different strokes for different folks; and all that jazz. Mmmm Hmmm

Speaking of which… Gimme some jazz and a glass of wine…

N-E TIME!

Mmmm Hmmm… like now

JAZZY SOUL #4:

Some jazz and …

a glass of wine?! Sounds fine

Lead me to it… I'll surely drink.

And don't be talkin all that jazz… jes play me some

JAZZY SOUL #1:

I can understand that. I can understand the marching and sit ins too. Still on occasion… I just want a good jazz tune to groove to!

JAZZY SOUL #2:

Yes, something about that jazz…

sooths the savage, integrates

JAZZY SOUL #3:

Who you tellin? Girl... don't it make you feel great... all down in your bones

JAZZY SOUL #4:

They tell me a young Miss Nina Simone

done wrote another one of them activist songs.
But... it is Jazz

DIRECTION: (all the jazzy soulz laugh)
Lil Momma Jazz walks over to center stage and greets the audience

LIL MOMMA JAZZ:

(Speaking to the audience)

Hey now Jazz lovers out there!

There may be some people out there... though I have never met **any**one... who may be unaware of what Jazz is.

Jazz is that real good, feel good

Way down in your bones and all up in your soul

Soothing the young as well as the old

You see... rooted in blues and ragtime; the Jazz genre of music came to be

in the late 19th century

and was extremely popular by the 20th.

Let me tell you all about the very experience...

Jazz originated in African-American communities throughout Louisiana. And yet, Jazz found it's **home** ... across the globe! You all know that music is universal.

It's a major form of musical expression.

And here's another lil tid bit of a historical jazz lesson

Ever heard of "active jazz"?

Of course you haven't... I just made it up

So it isn't likely that you've come across the expression

Anyhow, back to the lesson

Active Jazz is what I like to call Jazz fused with activism!

Here's an example...

You see Lady Day was singing about STRANGE FRUIT dangling from poplar trees, Nina Simone was singing about 4 women and telling folks all about Mississippi.

Remember the essence of activism known as Nina?

Oooh … now lil miss Nina… was an **amazing** soul.

She had a performance style all her own.

Her powerful performances captivated her audiences; all the while collaborating with Lorraine Hansberry to inspire young gifted Blacks!

Indeed… activism, social consciousness and contributions to music, as well as black excellence.

AUDIO CUE: A jazz groove begins softly Jazzy Soul Dancer enters stage right

DIRECTION:
*Dancer begins to dance and Lorraine Hansberry enters stage right

        LORRAINE:

    I am young

    I am a raisin in the sun

    I am the voice of Chicago

    Screaming from the stages of New York

    I am angry, loving, bitter, and proud

    Bookshelves across the globe will house my drama

    Awe Lil Momma

    My cigarette and typewriter

CUE: Lights down
Lil Momma looks up at the sky and hums as the jazz still fills the room

                    LIL MOMMA JAZZ:

    Lorraine

    Lorraine and Nina sure did inspire

    They empowered

    They were active

ACT 2 – THE JAZZY SOUNDZ AT THE JSC

AUDIO CUE: Jazz selection plays, Jazzy Soulz 1-4, and Lil Momma Jazz stage right.

JAZZY SOUL #1:

Ladies I don't know if I can continue our weekly meet-up here at the café. It is really getting dangerous out there… the civil unrest

JAZZY SOUL #3:

it's awful! I know what you mean

JAZZY SOUL #2:

Did you hear what happened?

JAZZY SOUL #1:

So much is happening; I've heard plenty. What is it that you're speaking of?

JAZZY SOUL #2:

They're calling those 9 boys, the Scottsboro Boys. People say they were set up.

JAZZY SOUL #4:

The papers say the woman on the train is a liar.

JAZZY SOUL #1:

My cousin knows one of the boys. Says he wouldn't hurt a fly or tell a lie to save his own mother's life!

JAZZY SOUL #2:

These times are really scary?

JAZZY SOUL #3:

Somebody need to tell Duke Ellington, Cab Calloway and Count Basie to write some new tunes.

JAZZY SOUL #4:

We need some big band pure jazz!

JAZZY SOUL #2:

Indeed! Cuz some savages need soothing during these times of chaos and confusion. We need some cohesion!

JAZZY SOUL #3:

I'm just glad that Jazz is here to Soothe.

The melodies of Jazz have brought us through some rough moments. A day of miracles ... the day Jazz was born.

DIRECTION: (all the jazzy soulz sigh and take a group sip of wine already placed on the table)

LIL MOMMA JAZZ:

(Speaking to the audience)

Be Boppers, Swingers, and Jammers

Gather round…

Let me give you a tidbit of the history of pizzazz created by Jazz

I just loves me some Jazz!

Well now that you know how active jazz can be…

Let's get lost in melody!

Wish old Louis Armstrong were here to validate…

After all he led the quest to facilitate

Jazz in the city of windy

Louis blew into town with that New Orleans sound

He played amongst the greats like Miss Ella, break that glass with her high pitch, Fitzgerald

I remember when I first heard that woman sing… sent chills down my spine. She sang my favorite song from Porgy & Bess…

AUDIO CUE: 1-2-3 Band plays intro for Ella, she reaches the mic, the band restarts the 2song JAZZY SOUL #1 aka Ella Fitzgerald   sings

JAZZY SOUL # 1 AKA ELLA FITZGERALD:

Now everybody knows **me**!... if you don't know ...
Then you just don't know.

Noted for my purity and tone;

I was known as... the **First** Lady of song!

LIL MOMMA JAZZ:

(Speaking to the audience)

Memories...

Jazzy melodies guided many to this lil café

Indeed...

My lil Jazzy Soul café has hosted many other notables in jazz that time forgot

But I did not!

What yall know about Miss Hazel Scott

Well everyone that knows Hazel ...

Knows how much that woman loved a foggy day

JAZZY SOUL #3 / HAZEL SCOTT:

Greetings Jazzy Soul Café, I am so pleased to be here.

I thought I'd stop in on my way from the train. This

café is one of the loveliest and my favorite here in the Puget Sound.

AUDIO CUE: Hazel Scott plays a tune...

DIRECTION: During Hazel's instrumental solo where there are no lyrics Lil Momma Jazz speaks

LIL MOMMA JAZZ:

(Speaking to the audience during instrumental break)
On Lenox Avenue

Where she grew into

the amazing pianist she's noted for today

they say... she got it from her momma

Hazel was a force... she could sing act and play

2 Pianos at one time

Sho nuff blow yo mind!

She stopped through here... brought her ball of talent to the Jazzy Soul Café.

AUDIO CUE: Hazel ends song

LIL MOMMA JAZZ:

(Speaking to the audience)

ladies and gents alike cleared the way

Whenever Lady Day

stopped in...

I hear tell Ella and Billie

were longtime friends.

I did take notice; whenever I saw one, the other wasn't too far behind.

I remember the time

Billie Holiday got punched in the gut at the front door of the café.

Naw now... Don't worry, we don't play that kind of jazz here... Lil Momma made sure he paid!

I lays the law down round here.

Anyways, Billie didn't miss a step in her stride

She never cried! God Blessed that child with high spirit and voice. That night, her choice?...

AUDIO CUE: At the words "That Night Her Choice" Saxophone Player gives the count 1-2-3 Band plays intro for Billie's song.

CUE: Dancer begins to dance.

JAZZY SOUL #2 / BILLIE SINGS:

AUDIO CUE: band fades music out Dancer stops dancing. Jazzy Soul takes her seat in the Jazzy Soul Café

LIL MOMMA JAZZ:

(Speaking to the audience)
Yeah back in the day

that lady surely had her way with song and anything else she wanted. She was a low key activist through jazz as well with her rendition of strange fruit.

Now that (she points at the audience) is a piece of Jazz history worth the research.

Lady Day's reign didn't end jazz's story.

We give Ms Billie her flowers and glory.

DIRECTION: All Jazzy Soulz clap

LIL MOMMA JAZZ:

Man! Nothing soothes like Jazz!

Every Jazzy Soul that came through the Armory station made their way to the café!

Listen… you could hear the vocals of Ivy Anderson, Aretha Franklin, George Benson, Gladys knight, and Sarah Vaughn too!

Talk about the jazzy sounds

We'd be prepared to do some thinkin

Anytime lil miss Abbey Lincoln

passed through

with her Afro Blu

AUDIO CUE: Band begins to play Afro Cuban beat

CUE: Dancer begins to dance.

ABBEY LINCOLN / JAZZY SOUL# 4:

Abbey sings and performs poetic verse

AUDIO CUE: *At the requests of Abbey the band softens music*

CUE: Dancer stops dancing.

ABBEY LINCOLN / JAZZY SOUL# 4:

An American

A Civil Rights activist

An Actress

A Jazz Vocalist

I wrote my own material

No water in my cereal

That sweet milk that quenched your thirst

Came from me

Pure and true

I offered my Afro Blue

LIL MOMMA JAZZ:

Art and creativity be the heart beat

Of this lil ole Jazzy Soul café

The Jazz sessions here irradiate every soul within
the this Armory station.

AUDIO CUE: BAND PLAYS the closing #

PROJECTION CUE:
Remaining slides should be of images and information related to cast,
band.

THIS PAGE IS UNAPOLOGETICALLY BLANK

ONCE UPON A JAZZY SOUL

AT THE JAM

Miz Portiontè Floes

AUDIO CUE:
Cue pre-show track
- **Aint Nobody's Business**

AUDIO CUE:
- pre-show selection ends ALL LAV mics live at this time
- ***cue for FEVER when Thelonious says CHOPS!

ACT 1 – KEEP YA CHOPS SHARP
DIRECTION:
An instrumental track plays (**Aint Nobody's Business**) and Lil Momma Jazz comes in after track begins.
Lil Momma Jazz enters *(at the Tin Lizzie) from the lower staircase area, she removes her coat and hat and places them on a coatrack, she then puts her apron (previously hanging on the coatrack) on and begins setting up the bar for service at the jam. **Upright Bassist is already present on stage and begins to play the Upright** (he plays a solo as id tuning his instrument)
As Lil Momma places on her apron, Dizzy Gillespie and Thelonious Monk enter (from the hotel lobby at the Tin Lizzie venue) as they enter they are laughing and making small talk.
At the same time... Coleman Hawkins and other musicians enters (from the rear of the Tin Lizzie venue) he chimes in on the conversation, yet more on the serious side about arriving on time to rehearse a new number before the jam begins.

AUDIO CUE:
The music fades / track ends after all characters / band members (except Cigarette Girl) take their places on stage at the instruments and Thelonious says... CHOPS!!!

DIRECTION:
As the track ends, cigarette girl runs in rushing with her cigarette box (from the lobby area of the Tin Lizzie). She begins speaking after Thelonious yells.

Thelonious:
Say fellas, I know Dizzy wants to blow that new tune
But before we shoot for the moon
Let's warm up to the sun
Let's get em nice and sharp
CHOPS!!!
Make it jazzy now

The Cigarette Girl:
Sorry Lil Momma, I had to pick up the cigarettes
Couldn't get the salesman on the phone
I forgot my cigarette box
so I had to go back home

Lil Momma:
Sweet biscuits and gravy... I don't do excuses young lady
Girl get it gear... folks still waiting outside to get in here!
Come on now

DIRECTION:
Lil Momma goes to the staircase on the side of the stage Tin Lizzie, as if to let folks know there will be a 5 minute wait.
The band begins to play FEVER and Cigarette Girl heads for the standing microphone as soon as Lil Momma heads for the staircase
  *****Cigarette Girl note:** *Pace yourself while the intro plays fusing with your cigarette box ... don't drag it out and yet don't rush to get to the mic sort of sashay looking over your shoulder for Lil Momma*

The Cigarette Girl:
sings Fever

DIRECTION: *Lil Momma Jazz reenters staging area, *out of view of Cigarette Girl, and silently observes the cigarette girl's unauthorized performance. *At the Tin Lizzie venue, Lil Momma enters from the real bar area to stand behind the makeshift bar. Lil Momma enters from the closet at 2+U*

`AUDIO CUE:`
- Band lowers the volume to dinner level when they see Lil Momma enter / If it is a track Lil Momma will enter when the track fades and the band will continue to play and come back in as rehearsed

The Cigarette Girl:
sings the outro to Fever
Mmm-mmm-mmm-mm-mmm-mm

DIRECTION: *Lil Momma Jazz makes her presence known and begins to voice her irritation with the Cigarette Girl also known as the café greeter / wait staff*

LIL MOMMA JAZZ:
What are you doing?!

CIGARETTE GIRL:
I'm just foolin around with the fellas Lil Momma
We gotta keep sharp
Ya know … get the chops warmed up for the Jam.
Gotta get these chops nice and warmed up.
Ba Ba Da Da Da Du Day (Scat)

LIL MOMMA JAZZ:
(chuckling)
Chile! Those are not your fans waiting out there.
I guess **aaaanybody** can dream though.
Them folks!... lined up waiting to get in here and … **drank**!

They done worked hard all day and they aint thinking bout your... feeever.
Your job **tonight**... is to sell those cigarettes you done got me to invest in.
Talkin bout how relaxing a cigarette is... how sophisticated a cigarette is...
You betta hope you sell some of those lil nasty things. Round here singing bout a fever. Folks need a greeting a seating and a drank!

LIL MOMMA JAZZ:

Are you done prepping that cigarette box, so I can get these drinks made?!
You getting on my nerves... givin me a fever! Go on and greet the gentlemen.

AUDIO CUE:

Band raises the volume to vamp to finale.

DIRECTION: As Lil Momma Jazz completes her tongue lashing she heads to allow entry to the jam guests; Cigarette girl makes her way to the entrance as well to greet jammers and solicit cigarette sales. The band resumes the FEVER instrumentation (softly) Sarah and Ma Rainey follow Lil Momma and CG past the band to be seated.

Jazzy Soul #1: **Thelonious**	All these cats been doin around here is rantin!
Jazzy Soul #2: **Dizzy Gillespie**	You got that right! Whole city's in an uproar! All... while going along with the program
Jazzy Soul #1:	Now hold on a tic ... the Minister got involved for sho when they beat that Muslim boy up over there across 110th street. I agree most hide in their homes and avoid the streets; but give Brother Minister and his followers their respect
Jazzy Soul #3:	

Coleman Hawkins Yeah them folks over at the temple handle things differently. As they say... different strokes for different folks.
Now a cat like me... I plays it fine and mellow. Give me some jazz and a shot of some smooth. By that I mean... anything that goes down smooth.

DIRECTION: *Jazzy Souls 1,2, and Lil Momma chuckle and take a shot.*

Lil Momma: Now that's groove! Some jazz and ...
a shot of gin! Lead me to it friend! (ha-ha) And don't be talkin all that jazz... let's jes play some

Dizzy Gillespie: I'm like Mr Clay, yeah
Gotta lil fight in me
I gotta make it swing!
That's my thing.

Thelonious Monk: Dizzy laid down this groove last week... called it Salt Peanuts.

Coleman Hawkins: Salt Peanuts! Salt Peanuts! Salt Peanuuutz!
We'll see if it makes the cut at the jam tonight

DIRECTION: *Everyone chuckles and takes a shot.*

Thelonious Monk: Say Lil Momma! ... What's the word?

Lil Momma Jazz: Hey now ... okay here's what I heard...

Last night... Beans & Cornbread had a fight
They tell me ... Beans knocked Cornbread out of sight
But they said somehow, Cornbread was alright

Word is… He told Beans to meet him on the same corner tonight!

DIRECTION:
Lil Momma looks at the audience and winks then looks back at the Jazzy Souls and shrugs her shoulders; as they realize she is only joking with them. They all laugh.

Dizzy Gillespie: Awww Lil Momma, I aint fooling witchu.

Lil Momma Jazz: Okay… Monkey, Coon, the N Word!...
Coleman Hawkins: Woe! Come on now Lil Momma

Lil Momma Jazz:

Just a serious response to the question I heard Mr Monk ask earlier…
What's… the word?
Growing up, these were amongst the most memorable yet painful… I've ever heard

Thelonious Monk: I'm sorry I asked Lil Momma

LIL MOMMA JAZZ: Chile aint nothing a lil active jazz can't soothe me through.

DIRECTION: *Lil Momma Jazz walks over to center stage and greets the audience*

LIL MOMMA JAZZ:

Hey now Jazz lovers out there!
There may be some people out there… though I have never met **any**one… who may be unaware of what Jazz is.
Well… rooted in blues and ragtime; the Jazz genre of music came to be in the late 19th century and was extremely popular by the 20th century. Those who've spent their lives living its very experience… tell me this genre originated in African-American

communities throughout Louisiana. However, Jazz found its home ... across the globe! They say music is universal and Jazz evolves. After all it is a major form of musical expression.

Now... What chu folks know bout some ... "active jazz"?
Well you see that's what folks here at **JSC** like to call Jazz fused with activism! There are many notables with regard to that active jazz.
Surely you've heard of Billie Holiday and her...
strange fruit.
And Nina Simone told **EVERYBODY** about Mississippi
You all remember Nina Simone don't you?
Oooh ... now lil miss Nina... was an **amazing** soul.
She was an activist, classically trained pianist, and a **truly** unique vocalist. She had a style all her own.
The things she did to captivate an audience...
inspiring!
She was multilingual as well.
I'm talkin fierce! **She was**! I say this Because...
of her activism, social consciousness and contributions to music, as well as black excellence.

AUDIO CUE:
Band plays 4 Women

Lil Momma Jazz sings

DIRECTION: *Lil Momma Jazz walks away from floor mic and begins speaking to the audience as the band softens the music to fade*
AUDIO CUE:
Band fades /Lil Momma's mic live again

Lil Momma Jazz:
    Now That's, "Active Jazz"
    Now when it gets so heavy that the jazz don't do it...

> I add a lil Gin Rickey cocktail and a Black Kat ...
> mmm hmmm now that'll do it!

DIRECTION: Everyone laughs, music begins to play, Lil Momma stands at the bar holding her long cigarette and looking upward as if deep in thought. She is also enjoying her cocktail and the music. Cigarette Girl sheds her box and takes her place at the mic to sing **Summertime**.

AUDIO CUE:
Trumpet and Bass begin to play an intro to **Summertime**.

LIL MOMMA JAZZ:
(talking to herself)
> Can't whip that Jazzy thunder
> I sits back, relax and I enjoy the jazzy reign

CIGARETTE GIRL: (speaking into the mic as music is playing softly)
> If anybody needs a cigarette with your Old Fashion or Gin Rickey... please see lil Momma. I'm gone sang me a tune now. Lil Momma if ya don't mind Ma Dame
> (she glances at Lil Momma and winks)

CIGARETTE GIRL: sings Summertime

DIRECTION: *BAND PLAYS solos etc or track plays til fade as the Cigarette Girl reclaims her box, and walks through the room and then out to the lobby area while saying Cigarettes.*

CIGARETTE GIRL:
> Cigarettes! Cigarettes! Lucky Strikes! Black Kats! Woodbines! Cigareeeetttttts!

Lil Momma Jazz: (speaking to the band)
> Oooh ... all that jazz
> How about it

You've been warmin up so long, those chops ought to be able to slice through metal by now!
It's time to put them chops to the test!
Yes!

DIRECTION: *everyone begins talking while summertime tune continues no one leaves the stage area but Cigarette Girl.

ACT 2 – LAYIN DOWN THE GROOVE with …
Lil Momma Jazz
Dizzy Gillespie / Jazzy Soul #2
Thelonious Monk / Jazzy Soul # 1
Coleman Hawkins / Jazzy Soul # 3
Cigarette Girl
Ma Rainey
Sarah Vaughn

AUDIO CUE:
The band lowers music to background volume (very low) when Jazzy Soulz 1-4 begin a conversation #1 says "The Civil Unrest" – Band / Track stops abruptly…

DIRECTION: As the Summertime plays Jazzy Soulz Thelonious Monk, Coleman Hawkins, and Dizzy Gillespie, exchange looks with one another, as
Lil Momma Jazz makes her way behind her bar.

Jazzy Soul #1:   Alright I'll say it… the civil unrest…
Thelonious

DIRECTION / AUDIO CUE:
Cigarette Girl Re enters as music stops!

Jazzy Soul #1:   is getting worse
Thelonious

Jazzy Soul #2:   I know you heard what happened yesterday?
Dizzy Gillespie

CIGARETTE GIRL:
           Cigarettes! Cigarettes!
           Cigareeeeeeeeeeeettes!!!! (drag it out and be
     very loud)

DIRECTION:
Jazzy Soul #1 looks at CG as if she has lost her mind then speaks

Jazzy Soul #1:

Thelonious

So much going on; I don't know what I heard man.

Jazzy Soul #3:
Coleman Hawkins

They arrested our Billie again; Got her on some heroin charges. You know it was a set up.

Lil Momma Jazz:

Oh no!
I thought the Lady Day was in the hospital; on her deathbed. This hurts my heart and head.

Jazzy Soul #1:

Thelonious

Last week the busted up the craps game in Ella's

dressing room. Got her the band and Dizzy!

DIRECTION:
Everyone looks at Dizzy as Dizzy Glares over his eye glasses at Thelonious

Jazzy Soul #2:
Dizzy Gillespie

Say what!? Mind yours fella! Mind yours.

Jazzy Soul #3:
Coleman Hawkins

I know Bumpy J had a problem with that!

Lil Momma:

You know it fellas! Why would the law even go in Ella's dressing room?! They don't ever bother Mr. Calloway or Lena Horne. Word is.. they call that passin.

Jazzy Soul #2:
Dizzy Gillespie

Now that kind of drama gets no pass. Guess nobody told the flatfoots...**Harlem is Bumpy's town**! They paid 4 that mistake!

Jazzy Soul #3:
Coleman Hawkins   I'm sure they paid more than Ella and the fellas lost in the craps game that night.

Everyone: Got that right!

DIRECTION: Dizzie blows his horn as if to make a statement. Lil Momma places shots on the bar for the fellas and shakes her head.
(*all the jazzy soulz sigh and take a group shot*)

LIL MOMMA JAZZ:
(Looking at and speaking to the café guests then speaking to the audience)

> I'm so glad that Jazz is here to
> Soothe. The melodies of Jazz
> have brought us through some rough
> moments. A day of miracles ... the day Jazz was born.
> Be Boppers, and Swingers,
> Welcome one and all!... to the place
> where you can hear jazz greats
> from many different states!
> Welcome to the Jam at the Jazzy Soul Café!

CIGARETTE GIRL: (smiles at lil momma jazz as she yells)

> Cigarettes! Cigarettes! 15 cents a pack!
> **Cig – a - rettes**! (drag it out and be very loud)

LIL MOMMA JAZZ: (shaking her head at CG and then smiling at the audience)

> I just loves me some Jazz!
> No really... Jazz and I are in a close relationship.
> Let me stop foolin!

> Now anybody who knows anything about jazz...
> knows it can be smooth
> knows it'll bee bop on yah
> Most importantly... You know it'll swing.

DIRECTION: The drummer drops the comedic beat(BA DUMP ADUMP),

DIRECTION: The trumpet player / Dizzie Gillespie, begins a tune that will play each
> time Lil Momma performs spoken word the entire cast on stage rock
> and sway to the tune until conclusion

LIL MOMMA JAZZ: (speaks to the band and they begin to play, she then directs her conversation to the audience)

> Many stop by the Jazzy Society Club for a good and heavy poor ... yet they stay for more!
> that soothing beat to make em move their feet
> a little crap shootin fun, a song from the Divine One.
> On the corner of Mercer on Queen Anne
> That's where we stand
> stop in and hear the house band
> we've been here since 1918
> not even prohibition interrupted this scene
> Ford paid the Seattle PD to ensure these doors didn't close... and everyone knows... MONEY TALKS!

DIRECTION: Dizzie Gillespie stops the tune and the cast stops moving

THELONIOUS MONK: This little oasis of jazzy entertainment for the hipsters, lovers, and jazz fans; has become a source of party for the domestic as well as the international. Jazzy melodies guided many to this lil café

DIRECTION: Cigarette Girl walks to staircase, stares at the crowd as she yells and stomps her feet. She exits toward the lobby left after completion of the yell

CIGARETTE GIRL: Cigarettes! Cigarettes! Ladies and Gents I've got 2 packs for 25cents **Ciiiiigareeeeeettes**!!!! (drag it out and be very loud)

THELONIOUS MONK:
(Speaking to the audience)

That baby doll really needs some help...
(shakes his head)
Someone please buy pack from her. Please.
I bought 2 already tonight. She didn't give me the
25 cent deal though
Come on ... help her out.

LIL MOMMA JAZZ:

Indeed Mr Monk... I'm a witness.
The Jazzy Soul café has hosted many notables in jazz. While time might have forgot ... I did not!

I remember the after-hours jam sessions that lasted til the sum came up; then that crazy breakfast crowd would rush in.
Everybody still trying to finish off shots of gin.
It was coffee with the Divine one, breakfast with Duke, Ella, and Lady Day. Sometimes Bessie Smith and Ma Rainey would stop in.
Good times!

Jazzy Soul #3

Coleman Hawkins: Lil Momma … who's your absolute?
Who's egg Lil Momma?
You know… Jazz's #1?

LIL MOMMA JAZZ:

Giggle water gotcha?
Or you tryin to get the fellas and flappers roarin?
A jazz favorite… I have not
I do have a preference when it comes to my shots!
(chuckles and looks at the fellas)
But **every** jazz tune… hits the spot
(Looks over at Dizzy G)
I see you wore your glad rags tonight… Got something special you wanna play Dizzy G? None of heavy pettin melody…make the juice joint jump!

DIRECTION: Dizzie Gillespie leads the band in a jam to honor Lil Momma Jazz's request… BoJangles joins in tap.

DIZZIE GILLESPIE:
(Speaking to the band)

Hope the chops are sharp.
Time to test out that tune 1-2-1-2-3…

AUDIO CUE: Band plays Salt Peanutz

LIL MOMMA JAZZ:

Keep em on their toes Dizzie!

AUDIO CUE: Band plays Salt Peanutz to end

DIRECTION: Lil Momma speaks to the Jazzy Soulz and the crowd. Ma Rainey enters the stage area and gets close to the mic, she walks over from the bar area where she has been mingling with patrons. Somewhere toward the end of the song.

LIL MOMMA JAZZ:

> Uh oh! The nerve ...
> Is that Ole Rude Getrude?
> Gents you at the jam fo sho now!
> While this one sings... no jazz
> She's got plenty pizzazz
> sets the mood
> here's your introduction to that moanin blues
> They call her ...

DIRECTION: Ma Rainey cuts Lil Momma off mid-sentence... screams her own name loudly as the band begins to play **Ma Rainey's Blues** (sound file included in email).

MA RAINEY:

> Ma Rainey!!!
> That's my name!

LIL MOMMA JAZZ:

> Let the music be your muse...
> Everyone the Jazzy Society is pleased to present the mother of the blues

DIRECTION / AUDIO CUE: At the words "Mother of the blues" Piano Player (Thelonious) gives the count 1-2-3 Band replays intro for Ma Rainey's Blues, written by Miz Floes
Dancer (Bojangles) begins to dance with Lil Momma Jazz, and Sarah Vaughn walks over and orders a drink from Lil Momma at the makeshift bar.

MA RAINEY:

They said they wanted somebody to spread the news
Wanted everyone to know... that feeling you get when you hear some good ole bluez
I heard the call
That's why I came
Hope you ready to hear me sang
Ma Rainey!
That's my name!
they wanted a brand new tone
I showed em how to moan
They wanted that Black Bottom sound
Ma Rainey!
Brought it to town
I heard the call
That's why I came
Here to sang the blues fo yah baby
Ma Rainey!
That's my name!

DIRECTION: /AUDIO CUE: `band fades music out`
`Dancer stops dancing.` *Ma Rainey takes her seat in the Jazzy Soul Café. Cigarette Girl Returns from near the bar area.*

CIGARETTE GIRL: (enters, glares at the Ma Rainey as she yells to the top of her lungs. She exits stage after completion of the yell)

Cigarettes! Cigarettes! There's gonna be a ban... get em while you can!
Cigarettes!!!! (drag it out and be very loud)

DIRECTION: The trumpet player / Dizzie Gillespie, begins a tune that will play each time Lil Momma performs spoken word, Bojangles begins to hoof *This time the beat is blues

LIL MOMMA JAZZ:
(Speaking to the audience as she shakes her head in frustration and directs CG off the stage with finger direction**)**

        Yeah back in the day
        Ma Rainey surely had her way with the moanin blues.
        She was often the life of our lil jam here; whenever she wasn't touring the circuit. Jazz babies let me tell you... Ma Rainey could work it!
        Record labels wanted that black bottom reverberation
        She brought it without hesitation
        Took the music situation to a whole new level
        She became the muse
        And so was born the Blues!

DIRECTION: The trumpet player / Dizzie Gillespie, stop
THELONIOUS MONK:

        Now Lil Momma
        You know I got a lil something you could use
        A lil chaser for that blues...

LIL MOMMA JAZZ:

        Oooh now what's that?
        What you got in your pocket ...
        I'm sure it's something with spunk
        Lay that groove on me Mr Monk

THELONIOUS:

        You know nothing soothes like melody... lil lady.
        Every Jazzy Soul that came through the café, left a jazzy stain in time!

Good friends of mine... Charlie Parker, Louis Armstrong,
Duke Ellington

COLEMAN HAWKINS:

Mr Monk you know your onions
You can't forget ole Sassy Sarah *(looks over at Thelonious)*
Mmmm hmmmm... Now she's the cat's pajamas
Talk about givin a fella a fever *(he blows a sassy note)*
Man those jazzy sounds swung through the juice joint daily!

Lil Momma:

(shuffles his feet as he speaks)
Ooooooh ... what I wouldn't give to hear the Divine One?

DIRECTION: Cigarette Girl enters stage right speed walking and speaking in disgust and frustration, rolling her eyes at Lil Momma and Coleman Hawkins... then exits stage left

CIGARETTE GIRL:

Cigarettes! Cigarettes!

DIRECTION: Sarah enters the café area and takes her place at the mic. Cigarette Girl continues her rant.

CIGARETTE GIRL:

Cigarettes!!!!
(drag it out and be very funny and extra loud)

AUDIO CUE: *Band begins plays the intro to Misty*

DIRECTION: Sarah gives Lil Momma a wink and gives Cigarette Girl a glare then begins to sing Misty.

SARAH VAUGHN:

        Sings Misty

DIRECTION: Band fades to very low as Sarah takes her seat, and eventually fades out as Lil Momma begins to speak

LIL MOMMA JAZZ:

    Sassy Sarah… Truly Divine
    I get misty whenever I hear that song

    Jazz be the heartbeat of this lil ole Jazzy Soul café
    The sessions here irradiate every soul within.
    We are pleased to be a portion… however tiny… of
    the song Jazz continues to create.

CIGARETTE GIRL: (enters stage area speaking in exhausted state and uses a pitiful voice)
    Cigarettes! Cigarettes!
    Is anybody gonna buy some Cigarettes?

AUDIO CUE: *BAND PLAYS the closing # - Strange Fruit and Lil Momma Jazz Sings*

LIL MOMMA:

    sings

AUDIO CUE: Band lowers music yet continues to play as Lil Momma speaks

LIL MOMMA:

    You know…
    Freedom, love, elevation, mathematical equations…
    all in there in the jazz!
    Well now folks… no time to dilly dally… head out the
    side entrance into the alley

Just a few minutes til the closing of the Jazzy Society. Fellas take us home

DIRECTION: Upright Bassist and Keyboardist play a jazz instrumental jam until the entire cast is on stage.

Thank You(s) acknowledgements and cast introductions here

(2)LIL MOMMA & (1)COLEMAN HAWKINS:

(1)Hi Dee Hi Dee Hi Dee Hi
(2) Ho Dee Ho Dee Ho Dee Ho!

Cast introductions, and thanks production support, band intros / solos / cast bows exits

AUDIO CUE: Band ends the closing # curtains

THIS PAGE IS UNAPOLOGETICALLY BLANK

ONCE UPON A JAZZY SOUL – er body n da club

ACT 1 – WHO'S EGG?

DIRECTION: Lights up as Genre enters from stage left. The band begins to play and dancers enter stage right. Genre joins in the dance with dancers and makes way to the microphone placed under the spotlight center stage.
When Genre reaches the microphone, the band lowers music to a fade and dancers leave the stage.

GENRE:

Who's egg

I beg... of you

Pick just one

They all sound superb

Ever thought of how it all started

What is was is what it is...

It's that pop... You know... that fizz

The hip, that you can't resist

It's that swinging be-boptastic smooth

Hey! Hey you over and out there!

I'm talking to you!

Well... I guess it is quite true

We haven't been properly addressed

And here I am, starting a conversation with you

Got the nerve to shout...

How could you possibly know what I'm scatting about

Let me try this again...

DIRECTION: clears the throat

    Greetings everyone and welcome...

    Genre, is the name I answer to

    It's a pleasure to meet all of you

    Well, now that the Segway is complete

    Please, allow me to repeat...

    It's that pop... You know... that fizz

    The hip, that you can't resist

    It's that swinging be-boptastic smooth

    That real good, feel good groove

    Mmmm hmmm

    (Looking up at the sky and smiling)

    Melodies that transformed times

    Once upon a time... Jazz was a peacemaker

    A bringer of joy

    illumination... for shaky situations

    Jazz was like a relaxing glass of top shelf scotch and a cigar

    Jazz is an easy chair

    Jazz continues to evolve

    But... once upon a time yawl

    There was a place where jazz thrived!

    This place was on the corner of melodic and smooth

    Located in the city of groove

DIRECTION: Band begins to play softly, lights Down, spotlight up on stage center.

Lil Momma and staff are setting the main room for the night's event. When Lil Momma begins speaking the music stops.

>> LIL MOMMA JAZZ:

Hey loves!

How is everyone doing on this fine day?

Oooh ...today is truly a special day!

I'm so excited I could just scat!

Oooh now... let me stop the madness

Lil Momma couldn't scat if she had an instruction booklet right out in front.

DIRECTION: She chuckles and holds her belly

Still I'm so excited, I feel like I just might burst!

It's Ella Fitzgerald day today! Yes ... the Cotton Club has made it O-fficial!

The house will be **packed** tonight.

It's nights like these... Madame Sinclair and Mr Bumpy Johnson make appearances,

I heard that pretty, little banana skirt wearing, Josephine Baker's in town

Sure do hope Mr. Bojangles stops through...

Tonight we need his copasetic view

Awww this joint's gone jump tonight!

And Lil Momma's gone make sure the Jazzy Soul Club is looking **right**!

I'm setting up, my new spot light!!!

I'm babbling... Come now, let's get the gears in motion

DIRECTION:
Lights dim / amber gel as Lil Momma Jazz walks over and unlocks the door or begins cleaning and other cast members (Duke Ellington is the 1st) enter set stage right

LIL MOMMA:

Well... look who the wind blew my way

on this fine and mellow day!

DUKE ELLINGTON:

As radiant as ever! You haven't aged a day Lil Momma.

Looking almost as good as me!

LIL MOMMA:

Duke you will never change. Still good looking

Still vain!

DUKE ELLINGTON:

Awww, you know you still the apple of my eye

Just be sure to leave room for an orange now

DIRECTION: They both chuckle

Word is ... Ella's making her way

Down **here** to celebrate her day

LIL MOMMA:

You hear true Duke!

I hear the cotton club is having a big to do…

Yet Miss Ella chose to jam with us *anyway*

DIRECTION: As Lil Momma Jazz speaks to Duke, Charlie Parker enters stage right
and greets Lil Momma verbally while tipping his hat to Duke Ellington as he
removes it.

CHARLIE PARKER:

Where's that jazzy looker?

Anybody seen Lil Momma?!

LIL MOMMA:

What's the word Bird?!

Always egg in these parts… Always!

I'm hoping you stopped in to jam with us tonight

CHARLIE PARKER:

Only if I can hear that amazing voice of yours

LIL MOMMA:

Well in that case… my ears are set for delight

With Ella stopping in to celebrate… there's no way
I'd miss out… I'll be jammin with the fellas tonight

DIRECTION:
Everyone chuckles reassuringly as Dizzy Gillespie enters stage right with Bill
Bojangles; these two are already in conversation.
Musicians already present on stage begin to tune / set up instruments.

DIZZY GILLESPIE:

Come on now pops! Why must we split hairs. You egg in my book, since way back.

We may not see things exactly the same. Don't mean either man is wrong. Difference of opinion is all.

BILL BOJANGLES:

Youngster… it just aint copasetic!

Gotta split that hair down the middle… like Joe Baker!

Let's keep it **all** the way copasetic.

Look here fella… the history of jazz… is the history of jazz!

Aint no opinions… Just facts!

LIL MOMMA:

Oooh… keep it mellow fellas

Now the actual fact is… Jazz continues to evolve.

That's real… it's evolving now and it always will.

DIRECTION:
As Lil Momma addresses Dizzy and Bojangles, Genre enters stage right. Lights on stage dim and spotlight up on Genre as Genre addresses the audience.

GENRE:

There may be some … though I don't cross paths with many… who are unaware of all that jazz really is.

Let's take a journey... shall we?

There are those who've spent their lives living the Jazz experience! And well... **they** know it originated in Louisiana.

Now ... While it is occasionally debated; where jazz originated...

Jazz would eventually find its home ... across the globe!

Yes... deeply rooted in blues and ragtime... Jazz loves everyone of us... a friend of both yours and mine...

it's color blind!

Most do agree that the time... was the late 19th century

Yet found true popularity by the 20th century.

Jazz is a major form of musical expression.

Jazz can be smooth, sometimes it'll be-bop on yah...

other times it'll even swing!

Gone jazz! Keep Doin your thing!

DIRECTION:
Lights dim, Genre exits, lights up on Lil Momma, as she takes a drag from her cigarette (on its cigarette holder).

                LIL MOMMA:

Now Uncle Bo, didn't you know… for a time, jazz even got active!

Ever heard of that … "active jazz"?

Sure you have!

That's Jazz fused with activism!

There are many notables with regard to that active jazz.

You've heard the Lady Day, talking about that… strange fruit.

Shoot… Langston Hughes', Weary Bluez… used jazz as a muse

You remember Uncle Bo…

when Lil miss Nina Simone would came along

informing us all of the happenings down south and especially in Mississippi. She wrote the 4 Women song

Well, that was jazz.

She used jazz to promote her activism

That beautiful, melinated soul had a style… all her own. Indeed she was young, gifted and Black!

Nina's activism, social consciousness and contributions to jazz, as well as the Black excellence, are to be forever cherished.

All hail Eunice Kathleen Waymon …

also known as Nina Simone

AUDIO CUE:
Lil Momma Jazz hums and sings what do they call me 4 times then speaks

LIL MOMMA:

What do they call me?

DIRECTION:
Cigarette Girl enters and begins to react to Lil Momma's spoken words

LIL MOMMA JAZZ:

They've called me many mean and nasty things…

These names neither belong to nor do they describe me.

Little Monkey, Darkey, Sambo

DIRECTION:
Cigarette Girl looks around like… I know she aint talking to me, then begins to prepare her cigarette box and chat with the fellas / band

LIL MOMMA JAZZ:

Strange be the black fruit

Dangling from that tree

Even stranger to see…

Mr Johnson with the other end of noose in his hand

Sad times on divided land

Then Jazz arrived… created bands and filled the stands!

Performers arrived on the A train

Jazz had plans

Plans to unify what was once divided

There was a renaissance … It was decided!

Jazz… was here to stay!

AUDIO CUE:
Lil Momma Jazz hums … what do they call me

LIL MOMMA:

What do they call me? - They'd better call me Lil Momma; unless they looking for trouble

DIRECTION:
Lil Momma Jazz looks over at Cigarette Girl

LIL MOMMA JAZZ:

Why are you late again?

This time the cigarette box beat you here!

The cigarettes were already present and accounted for

Now Bess… I will not allow you to stress me

Nope…Not today!

And no foolin around with the fellas

We must be ready for … First Lady Ella

and you know Lady Day will be stopping in

DIRECTION:
Cigarette Girl stops fussing with her box and looks shocked as Lil Momma continues

LIL MOMMA JAZZ:

Why you look so surprised

You know those two are friends

CIGARETTE GIRL:

First... apologies for my late arrival; no excuses for my abuse of your precious time

I'm *sure* that you will doc my dime

DIRECTION: Cigarette looks at the audience and then Lil Momma and continues

CIGARETTE GIRL:

As usual

LIL MOMMA:

You can trust that I surely will

CIGARETTE GIRL:

And not a tear will I spill... lashing from your tongue is well deserved

If I'm being honest, I feel a bit under the weather

LIL MOMMA:

Well you'd betta get it together

It's not the weather that you're under

It's my roof...

you would already know that If you weren't consuming hundred proof ... moonshine

Bess... get to work and quit wasting time!

DIRECTION:
Cigarette Girl straps on her cigarette box, Thelonious Monk enters stage right

CIGARETTE GIRL:

Ewww... heartless! Cigarettes! Cigarettes!

There's no jammers even here yet... but Cigarettes!!!

DIRECTION:
Lil Momma exits stage left, spotlight on Cigarette Girl, band begins to play melody for "Tobacco Tips", as she lookas around for lil momma and takes off her cigarette box, the band amps up her jazzy blues track

CIGARETTE GIRL:

Got me selling these cigarettes

When she knows I can sing

Old bitter and jealous

Because she can no longer do her thing

Once I shined in the limelight

Fame was truly mine

Then that man shook my career

Took my money and left me behind

It's a mess

Cigarettes! Cigarettes! Cigarettes!

Belly empty and pockets turned out

no record labels wanted me

still I've got talent ...there's no doubt

I might not have a pig's foot … no money for beer

still got song in my heart and I'm gonna sing it loud and clear!

Not sure how I ended up in the mess

Constantly causing me stress

Cigarettes! Cigarettes! Cigarettes!

Does anybody want a cigarette?

Band Solo

DIRECTION:
Cigarette Girl, speaks silently to the audience during the solo as if she is attempting to reach in the box and sell cigarettes, after the solo… she sings her outro cigarettes. Lights down at end of song as Duke Ellington and Cigarette Girl exit stage left.

Cigarettes! Cigarettes! Cigarettes!

She's always saying Bess… you betta sell some cigarettes!

Cigarettes! Cigarettes! Cigarettes!

Cigarettes! Cigarettes! Cigarettes!

DIRECTION:
Lights up… Lil Momma enters stage right.
Thelonious Monk enters shortly afterward and offers greetings

THELONIOUS MONK:

My Lady… Gents… Bess

Now I know that all folks

That's folks in every county… all try to play jazz

I say play… play your own way

Just make it good!

Cause *today* is Ella Fitzgerald Day!

DIRECTION:
Ma Rainey enters stage right as Lil Momma is singing Ella's praises

MA RAINEY:

Well big whoop

Ella aint nothing but a numbers runner

So what she can scat…

you don't think I can do that?

I started the Black music scene!

THELONIOUS MONK:

Ma… I aint neva thought much about race

Now you know music aint got no face

You moanin some of that good ol blues tonight?

MA RAINEY:

Got that right!

I'm jammin tonight, but for now I'm drankin…

pour me a pint Lil Momma

CIGARETTE GIRL:

Can I interest anybody?… Cig?! Butt? Bine? Cigarettes!

LIL MOMMA:

As you wish Mother Blues

One pint coming up

Fellas let's warm them chops up

Dizzy... how about some salt peanuts?

CIGARETTE GIRL:

Salt Peanuts Salt Peanuts Salt Peanuts Salt Peanuts!

DIRECTION:
Dizzy steps out front and counts off and begins to play

DIZZY GILLESPIE:

One – Two, One- Two- Three...

AUDIO CUE: Band begins Salt Peanuts (remix)...

ACT 2 – COPASETIC CABARET

DIRECTION:
The band (already present on stage) plays 1 swing jazz musical selection as Bojangles dances. Lil Momma has had a costume change and enters stage right as music begins with Ma Rainey.

LIL MOMMA:

I think I see Ella, Looks like everything is set

MA RAINEY:

Lil Momma don't nobody care but you!

I aint thinking about Ella! I'm ready to kick off this jam!

LIL MOMMA:

Yes mam

MA RAINEY:

Ma Rainey! That's my name.. and don't forget it!

DIRECTION:
The band lowers music to background volume (very low) as Bessie Smith and jammers enter stage right and take their seats off stage in the audience
While Ella and her entourage seat themselves at tables on stage, Bessie joins Ma Rainey

BESSIE SMITH:

Well now, I see Lil Momma spruced up the joint!
Yeah! First Lady of song in the club tonight!

LIL MOMMA:

That's right! Good times in the club ... Er body's here!

BO JANGLES:

Ladies and Gentlemen, Fellas and Flappers... The Club is now open! Welcome to the jam!

Introducing...

LIL MOMMA!!!!!!!!

DIRECTION:
The band continues to play Lil Momma greets the audience as Ella Fitzgerald and her entourage enters stage right.

LIL MOMMA:

Welcome one and all to the club. Look like Er Body's here!

If you didn't know, It is o-fficial

Today is Ella Fitzgerald day!

ELLA FITZGERALD:

Shots on me everybody. Have a good time!

MA RAINEY:

Ma Rainey! All Hail Ma Rainey!

But yo drank... is on Ella!

ELLA:

All hail who?! No one asked who you are!

This is my day! I'm the only star... shining here tonight. Correction... everybody but Ma's drink is on me!

LIL MOMMA:

Now ladies! It's all about a good time tonight.

You're both egg in my book!

Jazz babies Lil Momma shared with you earlier...

Ragtime and Blues pretty much got it on and birthed Jazz.

We've lost Scott Joplin so we can't get down on that ragtime this session

But Ma is here tonight to teach a lesson... about the Blues

Come on Ma and spread the news!

DIRECTION:
The band begins to play the intro to **Ma Rainey's Blues** until she reaches the mic at center stage. Then Ma Rainey sings her blues, and returns to her table at the conclusion of her song.

MA RAINEY:

They said they wanted somebody to spread the news

wanted everyone to know that feeling you get when you hear some good ol' blues

I heard the call that's why I came

Hope you're ready mmm hmmm... ready to hear me sing

Break it down...

They wanted a brand new tone

I showed em how to moan

They were craving that black bottom sound

Ma Rainey brought it town

Yeah I heard the call

Mmmmmm

That's why I came

Im here to sing the blues for you baby

Ma Rainey!

That's my name

LIL MOMMA:

Ma Rainey! The mother of the moanin blues.

So Now… **you know** the Empress must show the evolution

DIRECTION:
The band begins to play the intro to remixed version of Aint Nobody's Business. Bessie rises from Ma Rainey's table and takes her place at the mic center stage. She addresses the audience and then begins her song and returns the table at completion.

BESSIE SMITH:

For the misinformed… I want to make it clear

If I hear… ANYBODY

Speaking on my business… I will not hesitate… to cut you!

Song:

Hey miss lady

Mind yo business… stay out of mine

I'm trying to get somewhere

But for you I'll make time

I know how to be a lady

But I'm no stranger to actin a fool

See as long as you mind yo business

I can keep my cool

I see you lookin ova there

At that tall fine man

Well he's my business too

been doin my very best to make it plain

I don't think you understand

I'll try again to make it clear for you

I know how to be a lady

But I'm no stranger to actin a fool

You betta stay out of my business

So I can keep my cool

Break it down:

Get back woman

Don't make me ball up my fist

You'll get more than your feelings hurt

You got my britches in a twist

Band solo:

I know how to be a lady

But I use a switchblade … like a tool

You'd betta mind yo business lady

So I can keep my cool

LIL MOMMA:

Thank you for that bully Blues Bessie.

Whew!

I'm just glad that Jazz is here to soothe.

Sure don't want her cutting up in here tonight

Thank you for the soothe jazz

DIZZY GILLESPIE:

Be Boppers, Swingers, and Jammers

Seattle is the scene

to which Lil Momma's Jazzy soul clings.

This woman just loves Jazz!

Jazz is the actual love of her life.

Let's get lost in some melody!

Let's hear from the First Lady of Song

She fell in love with that Fella

Put your hands together for Miss Ella!

DIRECTION:
Chick Webb enters from audience with snare drum in hand, disrupting the audience during

CHICK WEBB:

Whatchu doin fella?

Let's keep it fine and mellow

Excuse me, excuse me

Could you move a lil to the left

She cant start without me!

She don't sing with **no house drummer.**

I'm the only one plays for Ella!

DIRECTION:
Band plays intro for Ella once Chick gets settled, Ella then advances toward and reaches the mic, the band starts the song Ella Fitzgerald sings "That Fella" and dialogue begins after the song

Song:

I'ts true, it's true, it's true, it's true

fell in love with that brown fella

He lied, he lied, he lied, he lied, he said

I love you Ella

It's such a shame

It's a crazy game

This old love thang…

Oh I fell, I fell, I fell, I fell

I fell in love head first

He quenched, he quenched, he quenched, he quenched

I swear he quenched my thirst

But he played a game

Aint that a shame

It's that old love ... that I blame

Vamp:

Oh he said he'd be

He said he'd always be right there

I believed, yes I believed him

When he told me that he cared

Doo bee doo bee do

Doo doo doo doo doo

Dwee Dup Dwee Dup

Doo be Doo bee Do bee Dee

It's such a shame

It's a crazy game

This old love thang…

ELLA FITZGERALD:

Now everybody knows **me**!... if you don't know … Then you just don't know.

I've always been noted for my purity and tone;

Ma Rainey... that's why I'm known as... the **First** Lady of song!

DIRECTION:
Ella ends dialogue, glares at Ma Rainey and then returns to her seat. Cigarette Girl enters from the audience area and returns to stage

THELONIOUS:

Miss Ella, break that glass with her high pitch, Fitzgerald

We've had the 1st Lady of song ... now we move on

she always sets my mood while in her solitude

Oh please won't you come have your way

Lady Day

CIGARETTE GIRL:

CIGS! BUTTS! CIGARETTES!!!

OH COME ON!!! OKAY down from 25cents per box to a dime! Only for a limited time! Special ends in 2 minutes! Cigarettes!!!

AUDIO CUE:
1-2-3 Band plays intro for Billie's song, she reaches the mic, the band starts the song No More Smack No More Gin

BILLIE HOLIDAY:

Come on now, support Bess purchase some cigarettes.

Umph! Er Body really is in the club

Some of us sang the same tunes

But... no two people on earth are alike, and it's got to be that way in music or it isn't music

Hey Ella! ... FIRST lady of song! Ha!!!

This tune's for... me!

BUT Imma sing it for my friend's celebration tonight. Is that alright?

DIRECTION:
Billie puts her dog down on a table and scratches and takes a sip of her drink and a drag from her cigarette and leans into her mic stand, the band starts the song No More Smack No More Gin

BILLIE HOLIDAY:

I don't have much

Still I cherish all that I possess I'm generous to the point of fault

Because I give in excess

One day my trauma will end

They'll notify my next of kin

No more smack... No more gin

I started so innocent, lost my way,

... so sad

Lost my sweet mother too

They say my Papa ... drove her mad

Someday I'll outrun the heartache

But until then

I'll shoot my smack... and drink my gin

The mighty thrive

The meek... struggle to stay alive

Juice and junk on a steady flow

When heartache's gotcha feeling low

No more Strange Fruit

It'll be a bitter sweet end

No more smack... No more gin

I'll be free to go

A lady... always knows her time

No more worries

I'll be fine

It'll be my final performance

My jazzy contribution ends

No more smack... No more gin

DIRECTION:
Billie returns to Ella's table

LIL MOMMA JAZZ:

Ah Billie!

That voice of yours is incomparable!

Hey Ella!

Jazzy melodies guide many to this club

Indeed... I've hosted many other notables in jazz that time forgot... I... did not!

While the weather got stormy... she stayed sizzling hot!

Fellas... Hell hath no fury like a woman scorned

Jazz had no other timeless beauty like that of Lena Horne

AUDIO CUE:
1-2-3 Band plays intro for Lena's song during her dialogue, the band starts the song It's Wet Ova Here after dialogue is complete

DIRECTION:
Cigarette girl rudely blocks Lena's path to the mic, yelling her Sale's pitch.
Lena Horne enters from audience area and sings It's Wet Ova Here after her dialogue is complete.

CIGARETTE GIRL:

Cigarettes! There will soon be a ban... betta get em from me while you can.

Can anybody hear me? I said... "CIGARETTES"!!!

LENA HORNE:

I made a promise to myself to be kinder to other people.

Greetings everyone!

I am so pleased to be here celebrating with Ella, Lil Momma Jazz, the Fellas... **AND BESS**

AUDIO CUE:
1-2-3 Band starts Lena's song and Lena sings to the song's completion and exits stage left back into the audience.

LENA HORNE:

He left me alone

All Alone and by myself

Stil I don't want

I don't want nobody else

It's wet over here

It's wet over here

I'm backstroking through my tears

Stormed out of my life

Leaving a fog in my mind

A puddle of pain

That's what he leaves behind

It's wet over here

It's wet over here

I'm wading my way through these tears

Bass Solo

After all this time

you break this precious heart of mine

Gave all that you asked for

the only man that I adore

Constantly crying

There's just no drying

These tears

Horn Solo

Its so wet over here

I fear I'll drown in these tears

LIL MOMMA JAZZ:

Someone please get Lena a handkerchief!

Is everyone enjoying Ella Fitzgerald day here at Da Club?

I remember a time, when a party like this had to be kept secret.

No interracial mingling was allowed.

DUKE ELLINGTON:

Men have died for this music

It's my mistress and she plays second fiddle to no one

CHARLIE PARKER:

It's your own experience, your own thoughts...
your wisdom

DIRECTION:
Lights down, Lil Momma exits stage left, Genre enters stage right, spotlight on Genre.

GENRE:

Jazz just keeps right on moving through time and space.

Ah, another familiar face... Miles Davis

AUDIO CUE:
At the words "Ah, another familiar face" Trumpet Player begins background music for Round Midnight poem.
Dancer begins to dance gracefully across the stage.
Spoken Word piece begins

DIRECTION:
spotlight on Genre as band plays music and Dancer begins to move to the cadence of the poet.

GENRE'S POEM:

Round midnight

That's when jazz comes tappin on my window pain

Melodies coming down in the droplets of rain

Your smoothness take my breath

You thump fizz and groove til nothing is left

Quenching my thirst like a glass of full bodied red wine

Jazz for you

I'll always make the time

Sway me to and frow

Within your melodies I grow

Passionate, purposeful, pleasured beyond measure

Your jazztastic grooves I treasure

I eagerly await each encounter

Round midnight

That's when jazz comes

Band Solos : Each musician solos here

Passionate, purposeful, pleasured beyond measure

Round midnight

That's when jazz comes

DIRECTION / AUDIO CUE:
Spot out, lights up, dancer and Genre exit stage left, music fades. Lil Momma enters stage right

LIL MOMMA JAZZ:

Man! Nothing soothes like Jazz!

Er Jazzy Soul that came through the Da Club embedded a jazzy stain within my brain!

When I listen close, I can still hear those amazing melodies...

CIGARETTE GIRL:

Cigarettes! CIGAREEEEEEETTTTTTTEEEES!!! Yawl don't understand; Lil Momma will fire me! Every week yawl come in and drink ... everybody buy one box and share em. Don't be cheap, support local folks like ... ME!!!!

Oh and do enjoy the jam. These musicians work hard and

Lil Momma don't hardly pay them **either**.

LIL MOMMA JAZZ:

Bess! You are testing the waters... you're sure to drown.

My apologies Ella.

GENRE:

Hey Jazz heads... I truly hope you're still having fun

At Da Club... they aim to please... and they're not done!

I just saw Esperanza Spaulding in Da Club too

Backstage with KEM trying to put together what they're gonna do

Whatever it is must include the talents of George Benson

Not to mention... Will Downing sitting back there with Rachelle Farelle! It's Ella Fitzgerald day and

Er Body's in da club

Talk about the jazzy sounds!

We just might run out of clock and have to stop

Before all of that ...

I don't know what I was thinking

I see this little beauty is ready **right now**...

Put your hands together for lil miss Abbey Lincoln

AUDIO CUE:
Band begins to play intro Afro Cuban beat

DIRECTION:
At the requests of Abbey all jammers join her on stage. As they enter center stage area, she hums and makes music with her mouth and then speaks

ABBEY LINCOLN:

That sweet milk that quenches your thirst

Comes from me... pure and true

I've offered my Afro Blue

The land that my soul craves

The land before the time of slaves

When was that?

The home that I run to

I rent from or purchased from...

you?

What can I do

Will my dreams come true

My shades of delight

When will they see the light?

This hill's getting harder to climb

Feel like I'm running out of time

Gotta carry the load can't loosen the grip

I must hold fast

tomorrow, today will be past

our future is at stake

tell me what... will it take?

There is a voice within me

Yearning to be heard freely

I shall convert it to melody

It lives in my soul...

I'll call it jazz

LIL MOMMA JAZZ:

Whew!!! Abbey Lincoln... always thinking

Well this... was a first!

Er Body N Da Club tonight!

But you've overstayed your welcome.

You've been here … all night long!

It's late and we are exhausted

Please… go home!

CIGARETTE GIRL:

For real! Yawl aint buying no cigarettes anyway.

AUDIO CUE:
BAND PLAYS the closing number and Lil Momma Sings

LIL MOMMA JAZZ:

It's been great

But it's getting late

I've gotta go home and rest my aching feet

I've had a ball

It's really been grand… That's one hell of a band

Yeah they're sweet

Now they're ready to tear it all down

You've ordered your last round

We've all had fun… no doubt

Still… you've gotta get out

Don't mean to be impolite

That just wouldn't be right

Not at all

We've shot craps, and poured the gin

We've celebrated our scatting friend

I've made the last call for alcohol

But now it's closing time

You're all good friends of mine

Er Body was n the club for sho

But now it's time to go

We all had fun ... no doubt

Spoken:
Now... Eeeeeeerrrrrr Body... GET OUT!

DIRECTION /LIGHTING /AUDIO CUE:
BAND lowers music. Lights out! Lil Momma and the entire cast exits stage left, excluding the band which continues to play.
Lights up full. Band brings up music and Lil Momma returns with cast stage right and intros begin.

THE END

THIS PAGE IS UNAPOLOGETICALLY BLANK

JAZZY BLUEZ ALL UP IN MY SOUL

Miz Portiontè Floes

FADE IN:

ACT 1 REMEMBER WHEN

Lights are very dim… with a silhouette *around center stage.*
Prior to the scene opening, slideshow plays via projection. The slideshow will include images of the Harlem Renaissance period,(people, places, events, the riots, raised homes & businesses, demolitions, homelessness, etc.), Harlem in the 50's and onward.
Lights up
The scene opens with "N" (dressed as a door person / concierge), walking onstage with a guest register in hand as jazz plays softly in the background. As he/she reaches center stage she/he addresses the audience, with a bow and tip of her cap /hat.

"N" AKA NARRATOR

Well hello theater lovers!

Welcome 2 the show

Please… allow me to introduce myself

Before this production begins

I will be speaking with you periodically throughout this production

My name is "N"

I'm hoping that you appreciate this jammin theatrical experience…
Jazzy Bluez All Up In My Soul

Now… some of yawl don't know nothing about that Jazzy Bluez

So here's some information

I'm sure you could use

Around about 100 plus years ago or so

Music... had a different groove

Sometimes a moanin blues, sometimes a jazzy swing

Those late night Jam Sessionz were the "in" thing!

Shoot, back then even poetry had a different flow

And Harlem? Well... that was the place to go!

The migration was great

Chile! Folks were coming from EVERYWHERE!

Chicago, the Southern states;

And all the way from New Orleans

Came one of Jazz's greats!

Lights dim / sound fades

Lights up
The scene opens with Louis Armstrong blowing his horn as he enters stage right. As he reaches center stage he recognizes that he is not alone… his tune fades as he begins to acknowledge the audience.

LOUIS ARMSTRONG

Musicians don't retire; they stop when there's no more music in them.

<u>What we play is life.</u>

If ya ain't got it in ya, ya can't blow it out.

Hello there! It's wonderful to see you.

I was just thinking to myself, blowing a tune, and reminisin about the days of old…

When that Jazzy Blues was all up in my soul

*Louis begins blowing his horn again and exits stage left. Lights dim then up again as N renters stage right and jazz begins again softly in the background.

"N" AKA NARRATOR

Ooooh… Just hearing Louis's voice

Makes the hairs on my neck stand up!

Now who dat comin now?

*Spot light comes up center stage, *the Spoken Word Artist has already taken her place center stage*
As spotlight comes up Spoken Word Artist begins singing the chorus of It Don't Mean A Thing

MIZ FLOES

It Don't mean a thing, if it ain't got that swing
Doo Wop, Doo Wop, Doo Wop, Doo Wop, Doo Wow

It Don't mean a thing, all you gotta do is sing
Doo Wop, Doo Wop, Doo Wop, Doo Wop, Doo Wow

Ah... Good times I am sure Louis can validate

After All he was literally instrumental

in the quest to facilitate Jazz in the city of windy... where he made it trendy

Louis came to town

With that New Orleans sound

He'd come to play

with greats like Ms. Blanch Calloway

I'm talking even before the days

When Minnie's Moochin

And low down hoochie coochin

Was on the lips of Mr. Cab Calloway

Yeah Louis set the stage and made many friends along the way.

Like Ella break a glass with her high pitch Fitzgerald.

Yeah times changed quickly though.
The Harlem Renaissance period ended
Some black folks were still singing on stages; some were being burned out of their homes, lynched on back roads, buried in mass graves, shot

Black folks went through a lot!
I kid you not!
The juke joints, bottle clubs, and basement jams
were fading fast

Live entertainment ... a thing of the past

If you knew where to look

You'd find that little nook

that feel good getaway

Like... Ella's Place

Now that was the spot

The session was guaranteed to be hot

Baby that joint was jumpin

jazzy bluez was thumpin

out the door and down the block

star studded jam sessionz

that hit the spot

Over and over again

A cool shot of gin

A secret game of craps

Between friends

In the basement of the joint

Made it a point

To keep the noise down

Didn't want the law comin round

This after-hours felt like home

Yet it was upscale and classy

And although Miss Ella could be quite sassy

She knew just how to set a fine and mellow mood

Ella would scat you out your shoes

At the Tuesday night Jam, Bessie Smith would sing the blues

The Divas cleared the way

whenever Lady Day

stopped in

Ella and Billie were **longtime** friends

Two of the heaviest hitting divas of their day…

If you will

Okay… here's the spill

After Harlem's Renaissance, the goodtime spots began to fade away

The world lost great masterful musicians, vivacious vocalists, amazing actors, dazzling dancers

Entertainment… like bad teeth

Started to decay

Now it really ain't nobody's business

But at Present… the once incomparable … "Lady Day"

Sits homeless on a crate

Where the doorway of Ella's once stood

And she really ain't lookin too good

Spirited beverages, her only friends

Vodka, Whiskey, Rum, Gin

Whatever she can get

Money she has not

When she isn't begging in her usual spots

She's resting up inside her cozy cardboard box

Still each day

She makes her way over to say hey

To her good friend Ella,

Who isn't there

But you'd swear she was

Because…

the conversations are so interesting

As one sided as they are

Miss Holiday sees herself at that bar

On a stool, legs crossed, cigarette

Chatting with the proprietor Miss Ella Fitzgerald

About the times of old…

When that Jazzy Blues was all up in her soul.

*Lights are very dim… with a silhouette *around An elderly Billie Holiday The scene opens with Billie Holiday sitting on a crate, center stage. Billie is acting as if she is sitting on a barstool, and sipping from a shot glass only visible to her. The Narrator speaks from stage left…*

"N"

Well now that she done provided the background

on where folks once enjoyed that Jazzy Bluez sound

Imma get yawl up to speed…

Yes Indeed!

So Ella has gone on to glory, and left poor Billie behind. Let me tell you… life has not been kind

These days the Lady sits outside the shell of a building that has mostly been bulldozed to the foundation.

One brick wall remains with the marquee that reads… Ella's Place

This was once the site of an after-hours establishment; owned and operated by none other than, Ella Fitzgerald!

Today… it's merely the shell of a building partially demolished and a homeless Lady Day sits outside talking to an invisible Ella Fitzgerald.

Alright now friends, this story begins with Lady Day posted up on her crate…

Just outside of Ella's Place

Where Lady Day definitely should not be!

You'll see why later

Now standing across the street

Approximately 20 feet

From Lady Day

3 teens

are in the process of

living their dream

They are rehearsing

about to audition at the Apollo Theater!

Lights dim

***Lights up 3 teens standing in a cypher singing "God Bless the Child"** *they will be positioned somewhere within earshot of Billie who is seated on her crate in front of Ella's Place*

*This scene will be pre-recorded on the street outside Columbia city theater and rendered on the projector screen at Langston Hughes.

GIRL #1

I'm nervous. I couldn't even eat this morning.

GIRL #2

Why? We stayed up all night singing. Girl we got this.

GIRL #3

I'm with her. Miss bubble guts ova here. I ate this morning and now I regret it. It's that last part that's got me kinda scared. I don't do 3 part harmony. Let's just keep it simple.

GIRL # 2

Quit it! We gon make Lady Day proud.

GIRL #1

Who?

GIRL #3

The bag Lady Day?

GIRL #2

Yawl are trippin! Yawl *really* don't know who she was?

*Spotlight up on Side Note who is standing off stage center in front of Billie

SIDE NOTE

(there is a ding sound… everything on stage stops, then the character sings in the key of E/C/A… pick one each time)
(sang)

Side Note!

(**spoken**)

Did you know...

Billie Holiday, born Eleanora Fagan, created a name for herself on the Jazz scene prior to turning 18?! Billie sang in night clubs all over Harlem New York before being discovered by John Hammond.

It was the year 1935, that Billie Holiday joined Count Basie's band and saxophonist Lester Young gave her the stage name of Lady Day!

*God Bless the Child was one of her signature songs

Lights dim
*there is a double ding sound... everything on stage restarts
*_Lights up_ 3 teens standing in a cypher
This scene will be pre-recorded on the street outside Columbia city theater and rendered on the projector screen at Langston Hughes.

GIRL # 2

Ok come on... let's try that last part.

(they start snapping their fingers and on into singing)
GIRL LEAD VOCAL

Them that's got shall get, them that's not shall loose

For the bible says and it still is news

BACKGROUND + LEAD = 3 PART HARMONY

Yo momma may have

Yo papa may have

God Blessed the child

God Blessed the child

that's got his o o own wone

GIRL LEAD VOCAL

That's got his oooooowwn

(real tight riff here)

Now let's go kill this Apollo audition!

Lights dim… *Spotlight up on "N" who is standing off stage center in front of Billie*

N

Hey new friends!

N … here again

Now here is where most folks would feel honored and proud to hear their songs being sang by the new generations. Yeah well… not Lady Day!

They just ticked her off in a major way. Just listen.

GROUNDSKEEPER

Every morning with this woman. Look at her; now she mad at the lil girls, over there trying to rehearse for their audition. More like jealous though.

(laughing and sweeping as well as heading toward Billie to ask her to move)

BILLIE

Now ain't that about a piss in a swingin jug. That's some sho nuff bull is what it is.

Aint nobody asked me NOTHIN!!! I can sing my own damn song!

(Billie shouts)

Ella! Ella! You hear that?

BILLIE HOLIDAY

Damn Sis... Look at us now. No teeth, sagging skin.

Ella! Where you at?

Damn... Look at this place. It's a mess. These stools need new cushions. Feel like they getting shorter too.

***(as she sits with her knees nearly in her chest on the crate)
*Spotlight fades and full lights up to expose the groundskeeper sweeping his way to Billie aka
Lady Day***

GROUNDSKEEPER

Good morning Lady Day.

Mam, each day I tell you that you can not be here.

They pay me to keep it clean and free of **any**... people. Now I know you walked in fame at one time and this was yo friend Ella's spot, but currently the powers that be, are demolishing this site and you have to stay off the property.

I tell you this everyday!

billie holiday

And you'll have to tell me again tomorrow! Get out of my face!

I am trying to socialize with my friend and have my drink (*she swivels on her crate and continues with imaginary Ella*)

Ella, would you please tell your employee I got a right to be here… I don't think the youngster likes me. I try to be respectful.

Despite how your place is looking now.

GROUNDSKEEPER

She's trying to be respectful?

Man… this old lady is a trip. Everyday with this… she lucky I know it's Ella Fitzgerald day today. She gone be salty when they finish the demolition tomorrow.

Go head on! Have your day… lady!

BILLIE HOLIDAY

Yeah and I will… That's why they call me Lady Day!!! Know that youngster!

See what I mean Ella? They aint got no respect these days…

Ha Ha Ha!!!… Like they had some yesterday… Bwaaah!!!

Shame… this place was the place to **BE!** Hell, the line to enter was stretched down the block and around the corner. After the Cotton Club and the Black & Tan, Ella's Place was it! Oooooh… this joint was ALWAYS jumpin.

You gave a strong and heavy pour, good plate of hot food, and a heaping helping of… on the spot, dirty scat filled, jamin jazzy blues sessionz.

Duke and Louis would grab a tune and make it dirty… and Ella, you'd get off in there and you would scat, Sarah would sing, and Cab would dance til the sun came up!

I remember Ella… I do!

Now… I don't know **how** I remember

Ha Ha Ha! I was VERY high in those days. Got my nod on regularly and drank a lil bit too. But I hung on in there! Literally sometimes. Ha Ha

Yep… and when I was good I was good!   I think… I think **(Billie nods off for a few seconds and returns to her slurred speech and babbling)** I was just born in a time when it wasn't hip to be my kind…

You know Ella, I could be up to my boobies in white satin, with gardenias in my hair and no sugar cane for miles, but I still sometimes felt as if I was working on a plantation.

But that music at Ella's… always brought me back to my inner peace **(Billie looks over at the woman who isn't there)**

Ella you just made it feel like home… the cookin, the scattin, the jam sessions that went into the dawn… and when Bessie would come down… Wheeeeewwww! That heffa and that Blues!

Ooooh she'd cut up? Ma Rainey taught that chile well! The two of em out there cutting a rug after Ma Rainey would get tipsy. She'd bend over to tap the floor… a mess! Bessie would drink your bar dry. But she paid nicely though.

It would just make my heart full when Louis and Duke would sit in… and Max Roach would go home and bring his drum set.

Just a mess, fussing with the crowd to move their tables for his kit…

SIDE NOTE

(there is a ding sound… everything on stage stops, then the character "Side Note" sings in the key of E/C/A… pick one each time)
(**sang**)

Side Note!

(**spoken**)

Now 1st of all… what was Max Roach doing there? Does Billie mean Chick Webb?

And lastly… this woman's name is Billie Jean Baker! –She ain't even really Billie Holiday. Our Lady Today is nobody famous. This woman done drank herself into oblivion.

The real Billie Holiday… died years ago! In fact the Jazzy Bluez All Up in her soul… was all made up in her inebriated mind. (***Side Note laughs heartily***)

This has been a side note

Lights dim
*there is a double ding sound… everything on stage restarts

BILLIE HOLIDAY

and when Cab would come in here with that Hi Dee Hi… good times…. Mmm hmmm

Shh*** It's almost stage time! I betta get inside and get my seat for the jam!

Lights dim as Billie fusses with her clothing to get it right for the jam. **Lights out.**

Intermission – Lights Up – "Minnie the Moocher instrumental" begins to play and intermission is announced by VOG mic backstage Slideshow of Actors / Actresses and their interviews is played during intermission along with slideshow of the characters they are portraying and the Harlem Renaissance, Riots etc.

FADE IN:

ACT 2 IF IT AINT GOT THAT SWING

Lights up (two mics on straight stands for vocalist and horn, band set-up boom mic for keys (drummer, Duke Ellington, upright bassist, Louis Armstrong) Band is present minus the drummer and kick drum is also missing, dancers are on the dance floor laughing and creating a routine

NARRATOR

Welcome to the Jam yawl!

This here is Ella's Place

and things are already in full swing tonight.

We step on the scene just in time to witness a Ella Fitzgerald standing in irritated state behind the bar, facing Billie Holiday who is seated on barstool #1, with a glass of scotch clutched in one hand and a cigarette in the other.

Seated on barstool #2, being served a martini by Ella is the Divine 1, miss Sarah Vaughn… and standing between barstools #1&2 stood the root of Ella's frustration, the Empress… Bessie Smith.

Lawd… Bessie is sho nuff clowin as usual. She has her money in fist, and is giving Ella the what for! The Cigarette Girl is patrolling the floor and…

Off in the distance there is a table with no light on it... where Ma Rainey should be seated. However she is dancing in the isles as she loudly sings above the music and off key!

CIGARETTE GIRL

Cigarettes! Who needs a cigarette?!

I got those new filtered cigarettes!

ELLA FITZGERALD

At least once a month!

we gotta travel this road Bessie... not tonight. Chile please!

BESSIE SMITH

It's a long old road, but I know I'm gonna find my gin at the end.

I spend too much money fa you to be actin funny now

ELLA FITZGERALD

And I appreciate your business sistah, but you cannot drink up all my liquor tonight Bessie. I got a packed house!

BESSIE SMITH

Well send somebody to restock! *(Bessie extends cash to Ella)* I'm drinking tonight Ella! Come on now... Just give me a damn bottle woman!

MA RAINEY

Ma Rainey! That's my name!

ELLA FITZGERALD

Why you gotta clown all the time Bessie… damn! *(Ella laughs hearty, takes the money from Bessie's hand and hands Bessie a full unopened bottle of liquor)*

CIGARETTE GIRL

Miss Bessie, Miss Ella…

Yawl want a cigarette?

I see yawl already got the fire!
You know I got those new filtered kind
(chuckling…)

SARAH VAUGHAN

(chuckling…) The Empress is in the building! Gettin some Blues tonight! Yes!

(there is a ding sound… everything on stage stops, then the character "Side Note" sings in the key of E/C/A… pick one each time)

SIDE NOTE

(sang)

Side Note!

(spoken)

Did you know…

Duke Ellington's last words were…

Music is how I live, why I live and how I will be remembered.

Born in 1899, Edward Kennedy "Duke" Ellington, was the greatest jazz composer and bandleader of his time. One of the originators of big-band jazz, he led his band for more than 50 years and composed thousands of scores

No one in the history of jazz expressed himself more freely; or with more variety, swing, and sophistication than Duke Ellington did.

Lights dim
***there is a double ding sound… everything on stage restarts**
Band begins to play Minnie the Moocher groove as **Cab Calloway Dances for 60 seconds and sings Folks let me tell you bout Minnie the Moocher she was a low down Hoochie Coocher…** *the Cab says "ssshhh", the music softens and lights dim and spot light shines on Duke Ellington.*

DUKE ELLINGTON

Good evening… welcome to Ella's Place.

There are two kinds of music. Good music, and the other kind. You'll only find the good kind here.

The common root, of course, comes out of Africa. *(African drum beat track plays here and dancers come out dressed as ancient tribal dancers and dance to the drum beat, then after 60 seconds dancers exit, drum track stops, and Duke continues speaking)* That's the pulse. The African pulse! It's all the way back from . . . the old slave chants and up through the blues, jazz, and up through rock. It's all got the African pulse.

***as the beautiful melodic tones from the keyboards are playing Ma Rainey yells over Duke Ellington speaking…**

MA RAINEY

Ma Rainey! That's my name! I brought ya that bluez baby!

DUKE ELLINGTON

Ha Ha!
That's facts!

*Beautiful melodic tones from the keyboards for about 4 bars then Duke continues speaking

Now Hip Chicks and Cool Catz… the Lady is in the house tonight
Lady Day… please join us

LOUIS ARMSTRONG

Oh Yeeeaaahhh (*in his raspy singing voice*)

BILLIE HOLIDAY

Thank You Duke…
You know Louis… I think I copied my style from you. Because I used to like the big volume and the big sound that Bessie got when she sang … and I liked the big feeling that I got when you'd blow your horn.
But I found that it didn't work with me, because I didn't have a big voice. So anyway between the two of you… I sort of got Billie Holiday.
(*she smiles at Louis and then at the audience*)

*Billie then sings a song and exits stage and returns to bar stool

==duke ellington==

>Always a lady!

>Remember Billie... Be a number one yourself. Not a number two somebody else.

>Let's keep this jelly rollin and keep your applause roaring for the Empress of Blues...

>Bessie Smith!

>Here to cut up and take names...

(there is a ding sound... everything on stage stops, then the character "Side Note" sings in the key of E/C/A... pick one each time)

==SIDE NOTE==

>**(sang)**

>Side Note!

>**(spoken)**

>Did you know...

>Bessie Smith was nicknamed the "**Empress of the Blues**"? She was the most popular female blues singer of the 1920s and 1930s.

>As a youth Bessie was hired as a dancer for a traveling troop... despite the fact that she'd auditioned as a singer; because Ma Rainey, was already the troop's singer.

>By the 1920s, she had established herself in the South and along the East Coast.

>Bessie was signed to Columbia Records, became the highest-paid black entertainer and began traveling in her own 72-foot-long railroad car!

She received the nickname of 'Queen of the Blues', but the press upgraded her to the 'Empress of the Blues'.

But chiiiiile (child) When Bessie's career took a dive, she was booked as the second artist in a show and had to work as a cigarette salesgirl in the audience between acts.

No jive... this was a loooong side note! Had to hold that one a while... Whew!(*she says as if winded*)

Lights dim
*there is a double ding sound... everything on stage restarts

BESSIE SMITH

(*Yelling at someone in the audience*)

And Didn't nobody ask her for it!

I done told you to mind yo business!!!

(*Bessie takes the stage with a drink in her hand speaking into the mic as it is on the stand*)

Look here **Dook ... E**...

I aint gone cut up this time

I might cut somebody (she looks as Duke jokingly)

Naw, I promised Ella I'd be worthy of my title tonight. I am the Empress (she says with her head tilted toward the ceiling and with arrogance)

*Just as Bessie looks toward the ceiling... the drummer who has previously left the stage is making his way back through the audience with a snare and stand...)

CHICK WEBB

(Fussing through the crowd making a clumsy nuisance of himself)

Excuse me, can you make room, trying to get to the stage, excuse me please done told you to mind yo business!!!

BESSIE SMITH

Tonight I wanna remind folks, how important it is to mind their business (*she sips from her glass and glares at Max Roach*)

Oh, and Chick … unlike Ella, I don't want no drummer! I sets my own tempo.

(there is a ding sound… everything on stage stops, then the character "Side Note" sings in the key of E/C/A… pick one each time)

SIDE NOTE

(**sang**)

Side Note!

(**spoken**)

Now the drummer Miss Bessie is speakin so rudely to is, none other than… Chick Webb! Now Bessie has truly crossed the line. She has disrespected the "Savoy King"! Chick Webb was the sho nuff of drummin; he began playing **professionally** at the age of 11! Chick had that "new swing" style and his band was the "house band" at the Savoy Room. Chick was like 17 then. Bessie needs to stop. She just mad at Ella and takin it out on her buddy Chick.

Lil side note for ya

Lights dim
*there is a double ding sound… everything on stage restarts

<mark>CHICK WEBB</mark>

(Yelling from stage rear as he sets his snare on the stand)

Well, I aint goin nowhere! Once I set these up… I'm here all night! Woman talkin all that jazz; aint gone give me the bluez

You something Bessie, someday I'm gonna be walkin' up the street one way and you're gonna be comin' down the other way…

<mark>DUKE ELLINGTON</mark>

(Interrupting the argument about to start) Now Empress… this drummer, only follows two rules!

Number 1- Never quit and Number 2 – Never forget rule Number 1

*Drummer (ba dun da dun)

<mark>BESSIE SMITH</mark>

Ha! Ha! I know that's the truth

Because, the Greatest Blues Singer in the World Will Never Stop Singing.

(She says as she points to herself)

<mark>MA RAINEY</mark>

Ma Rainey! That's my name! Kiss my bluezy black bottom!

Bessie laughs hearty and then sings a song
as Bessie exits the stage, cab enters the stage, the mic changes hands as they cross

CAB CALLOWAY

Bessie… you sho know how to lay into a groove!
Duke, Louis… let's lay down groove…

DUKE ELLINGTON

Cat we been layin down grooves all night!

What you got Satchmo?

LOUIS ARMSTRONG

Every time I close my eyes blowing that trumpet of mine, I look right into the heart of good old New Orleans. And I think to myself… What a wonderful world (**band begins to play what a wonderful world**)

CAB CALLOWAY

Hi Dee Hi Dee Hi Dee Hi, O Dee O Dee O Dee O… At this time I'd like to invite the Divine 1 to join us…

(there is a ding sound… everything on stage stops, then the character "Side Note" sings in the key of E/C/A… pick one each time)

SIDE NOTE

(**sang**)

Side Note!

(**spoken**)

Did you know…

Throughout her career, Miss Vaughan was affectionately known as Sassy or the Divine Sarah. The first nickname reflected her sense of humor and the mischievous sexiness that often inflected her singing and stage patter. … Sarah

Lois Vaughan was born in Newark, on March 27, 1924.

Ella Fitzgerald called her the world's "greatest singing talent." During the course of a career that spanned nearly fifty years, Sarah Lois Vaughan was the singer's singer, influencing vocalists of many age groups, ethnic backgrounds, etc. She was among the musical elite identified by their first names.

She was Sarah, Sassy — the incomparable Sarah Vaughan, and of course… the Divine One.

As the 1940s gave way to the 1950s, Sarah expanded her jazz repertoire to include pop music. While jazz purists balked at these efforts, no one could deny that in any genre, the Divine 1 had one of the greatest voices in the business.

Lights dim
*there is a double ding sound… everything on stage restarts
Lights up and music starts as Sarah makes her way to the stage…
FEVER is played softly in the background, and Cab does a little dance on stage

<mark>SARAH VAUGHAN</mark>

Alright now Fellas, I don't wanna complicate it by thinking about it… you know I never do it the same way anyhow.
*The music begins to play softly
You know Satchamo… Horns always influenced me… more than voices!
This one's for you (Sarah points to the crowd)
Sarah then sings a song
* Cab Calloway returns to the stage just at the end of Sarah's performance… Duke Ellington and the band begin to jam an uptempo tune softly as ambience for Cab's lines
<mark>CAB CALLOWAY</mark>

Sistah Sarah … Pass that thing, slightly, lightly and politely.

You know folks... a movie and a stage show are two entirely different things. A movie picture, you can do anything you want... you can cut out a scene, put in a scene, whatever you want. They don't do that on stage.

It's all jamin and jivin in here...

Everybody did something. It was very entertaining. We had a lot of fun. And there was no segregation!

(there is a ding sound... everything on stage stops, then the character "Side Note" sings in the key of E/C/A... pick one each time)

SIDE NOTE

(**sang**)

Side Note!

(**spoken**)

Did you know...

Cab Calloway swiped the name Minnie the Moocher from his older sister's song Growlin Dan? Yes Minnie was a character in that song. In fact, Cab's style was similar to that of his older sister's, Blanche Calloway, African American Orchestra leader.

Cabell Calloway III, was a native of Rochester, New York born December 25, 1907. He was an Iroquois African American bandleader, singer, and all-around entertainer!

a master of energetic scat singing, Cab Calloway swung into stardom with his performances at the Cotton Club and his song "Minnie the Moocher" (1931).

Cab was known for his frenzied movements, signature white tuxedo and tails, and audience sing-alongs. His Cotton Club radio broadcasts and radio appearances with Bing Crosby made him one of the wealthiest performers during the Depression era.

He possessed an exuberant performing style and led one of the most highly regarded big bands of the swing era in the United States, from the early 1930s to the late 1940s.

He also appeared in films.

Lights dim
***there is a double ding sound… Lights up everything on stage restarts**

All night long, song after song, that hip chick served drink after drink
Now I think…
After all that
We could all use a scat
Ella get on up here!

** Cab Calloway hits the dancefloor and begins to dance as Ella makes her way to the vocal mic and begins to scat freestyle for approx. 60 seconds*

***Band begins to play a song** and Ella sings and scats after her dialogue*

<mark>ELLA FITZGERALD</mark>

"Once, when we were all playing at the Apollo, Miss Billie Holiday was working a block away at the Harlem Opera House.

(Ella Points to Billie on the barstool, Billie throws her hand up to tell Ella to hush, Ella then looks at the band and crowd as she continues speaking)

Some of us went over between shows to catch her, and afterwards we went backstage. I did something then, and I still don't know if it was the right thing to do - I asked her for her autograph."

(there is a ding sound… everything on stage stops, then the character "Side Note" sings in the key of E/C/A… pick one each time)

SIDE NOTE

(**sang**)

Side Note!

(**spoken**)

Did you know…

Ella Fitzgerald is known as the First Lady of song?!

Ella set the stage for many of today's stars. She accomplished a great deal during the course of her career.

She also overcame many instances of discrimination. She was a true powerhouse and left behind an amazing legacy! Her recording of ***A Tisket A Tasket*** skyrocketed her career by selling 1 million copies! It stayed on the charts for 17 weeks. She was the 1st African American woman to receive multiple Grammy awards at **the very 1st** ceremony in 1958. Ella won 14 Grammys throughout her career, and was also honored with the Lifetime Achievement Award in 1967. If that don't move yah… she was one of the first stars to perform during the Super Bowl halftime show in 1972.

On the flip side… Ella was also a runner for local gamblers, (picking up bets and dropping off money)

Once Police arrested band members in Ella's dressing room for shooting dice!

What was the law doing in that woman's dressing room? Talk about discrimination!

To top it off... after they got Ella down to the station, they asked for an autograph!

Despite segregation and discrimination... Ella became the first African American woman to headline at Manhattan's infamous Copacabana!

(Lil Miss Side Note skats here)
Lights dim
***there is a double ding sound… everything on stage restarts**
***(Music begins to play here)**
***Ella sings If it ain't got that swing**
***(music is a light hum here… plays softly as Ella speaks)**

ELLA FITZGERALD

Ladies and Gentlemen… thank you so much for stopping in tonight for the afterhours jam! We've done it again… Sun's coming up… It's closing time.
"Where there is love and inspiration, I don't think you can go wrong."
***(Music gets amped up… If it aint got that swing)**
Divine 1, Empress, Lady Day; thank you for sharing with us tonight. What a show up and show out kind of night this was!

***Spot shines on table in the distance**
MA RAINEY

(speaking very loudly over the music and Ella)

Wait just a damn minute!… Get it right!

***Music stops abruptly! *Spot shines on "N"**

ELLA

(speaking respectfully yet stern)

Now Ma... I respect you as my elder an all; but you in my spot... mind yo tongue now!

"N" / NARRATOR

Uh Oh, Now Ma is feeling disrespected! After all she was rejected!

Well she done said her name all night long

Before and after EVERY song

How they gone forget MA RAINEY?

She showed them all the ropes!

Anyways... back to the story yawl

The drama has begun

CIGARETTE GIRL

Oooooh! Anybody need a cigarette?

Yawl know I got that new filtered kind
(she looks around the room)
Well I'm gone have one... This is gone be a good one!

(there is a ding sound... everything on stage stops, then the character "Side Note" sings in the key of E/C/A... pick one each time)

SIDE NOTE

(sang)

Side Note!

(spoken)

Ma Rainey was dubbed "the Mother of the Blues"

born Gertrude Pridgett in 1886,   Ma Rainey was the first popular stage entertainer to incorporate authentic blues into her song repertoire

She began her career at the early age of 14. She got her start performing with Black minstrel troupes in roaming "tent shows" at the turn of the century!

There was an extensive minstrel circuit of Black performers.

Ma's big, deep voice was unusual in a girl so young. This made her a popular attraction in any show she joined.

What most captured her audiences' attention was Ma's voice, which by all accounts was huge and commanding. When she sang a "moaning" song, which would soon be referred to as **blues**, she could captivate a room in no time at all.

Ma opened the door for Bessie Smith and many others!

A much needed side note… and my last

(she laughs as she bellows a bluezy side note)
Lights dim
***there is a double ding sound… everything on stage restarts**
***(Music begins to play here)**

<mark>MA RAINEY</mark>

(speaking very loudly)

Wait just a damn minute!…
<mark>ELLA</mark>

(frustrated and intoxicated)

Ooooh! I know she aint still yelling up in MY HOUSE!

MA RAINEY

(speaking very loudly over Ella)
Get it right!
All this Ella this, Billie that, Empress, Divine 1.... I started allllll this!

This here be an empty world without the blues. A tune is like a staircase... Walk up on it! *(the **band begins to play as Ma Rainey continues her dialogue)**

Yeah… They hear it come out, but they don't know how it got there. They don't understand that's life's way of talking. You don't sing to feel better. You sing cause that's a way of understanding life.
Baby... I let my soul do the sangin'

ELLA

(frustrated and intoxicated)

Duke keep that blues goin so Ma can sing and I can go home!

Come on tell em a lil something Ma!

(Ma Rainey Sings)
They said they wanted somebody to spread the news
Wanted everyone to know... that feeling you get when you hear some good ole bluez
I heard the call
That's why I came
Hope you ready to hear me sang

Ma Rainey!
That's my name!
they wanted a brand new tone
I showed em how to moan
They wanted that Black Bottom sound
Ma Rainey!
Brought it to town
I heard the call
That's why I came
Here to sang the bluez fo yah baby
Ma Rainey!
That's my name!

(music fades as Ma speaks her last lines)

MA RAINEY

All hail

Ma Rainey!

(Ma Rainey says while taking the last sip of her drink and toasting the crowd)
Black Out Lights… Louis Armstrong "what a wonderful world" plays
*Lights Black out Spot shines on Billie seated back on the crate)

ELLA FITZGERALD

(Chuckles via background backstage mic as if speaking from the Heavens)…
Good Times, Good Times

BILLIE HOLIDAY

(Chuckles Loudly)… Ah Memories
The whole basis of singing is feeling. Unless I feel something, I can't sing.
That Jazzy Blues! All Up in my soul.
Ah see now that's… my thing.
Come here baby! (said loudly)

I think I will have one of those cigarettes! (spoken in normal tone)

***Lights dim** in the distance the cigarette girl is heard shouting… Cigarettes! I got them new filtered kind!(spoken from backstage) a projected slideshow plays as Billie lifts her crate from stage right and travels toward her cardboard home.*
As she walks she stops frequently to intake the sights shown on the projection screen… she never upstages the slideshow)

*LIGHTS FULL! / FINALE BEGINS

ENTIRE CAST COMES ON STAGE… ONE BY ONE IN ORDER OF APPEARANCE… SINGING
(**Enter stage right, singing and moving to far stage left, so as to provide space for other cast members**)

THE END

MY BLAQUE THEATER
A THEATER ANTHOLOGY

MIZ PORTIONTÉ FLOES
©2024
PAu 4-230-657

MESSAGE FROM THE AUTHOR

I believe the fusion of poetry and theater is a great source of mental nourishment, as well as an excellent platform to exhibit imagination.

My Blaque Theater, is an innovative style anthology of my theater productions; a refreshing splash into the world of Spoken Word performance.

What started as poetic verse; morphed into theater. I visualized scenes and heard music. My imagination took over!

For 10 plus years I've worked diligently, to "liven up" my Spoken Word performances.   The overall goal has always been... to provide underserved communities with positive and educational entertainment.

I hope that you've enjoyed MY BLAQUE THEATER.

Mix Floes

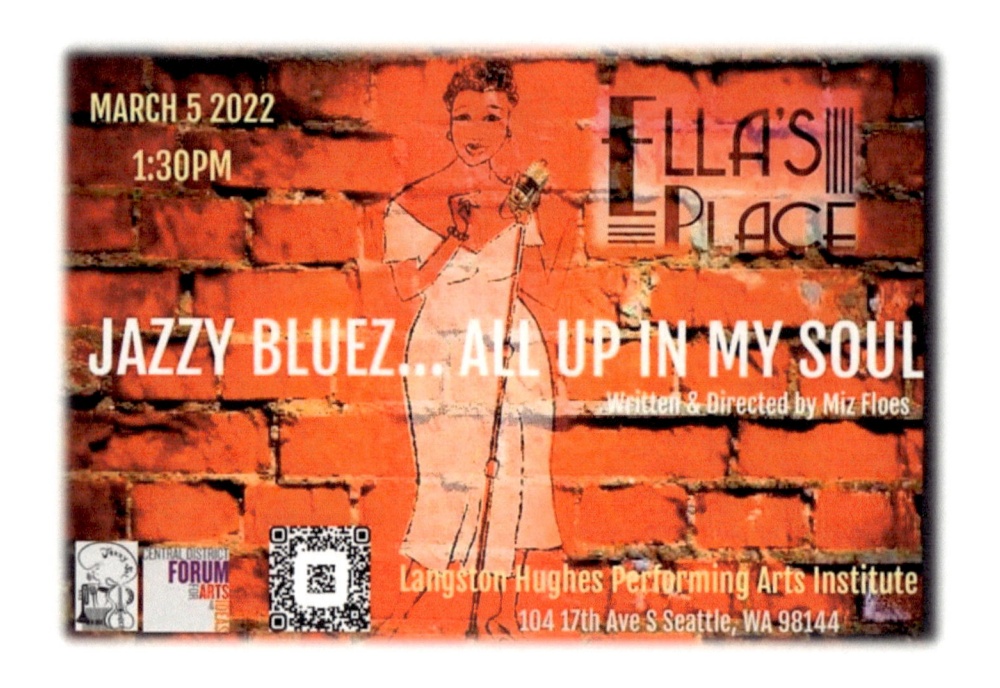

JAZZY BLUEZ ALL UP IN MY SOUL

ONCE UPON A JAZZY SOUL AT THE JAZZY SOUL CAFÉ

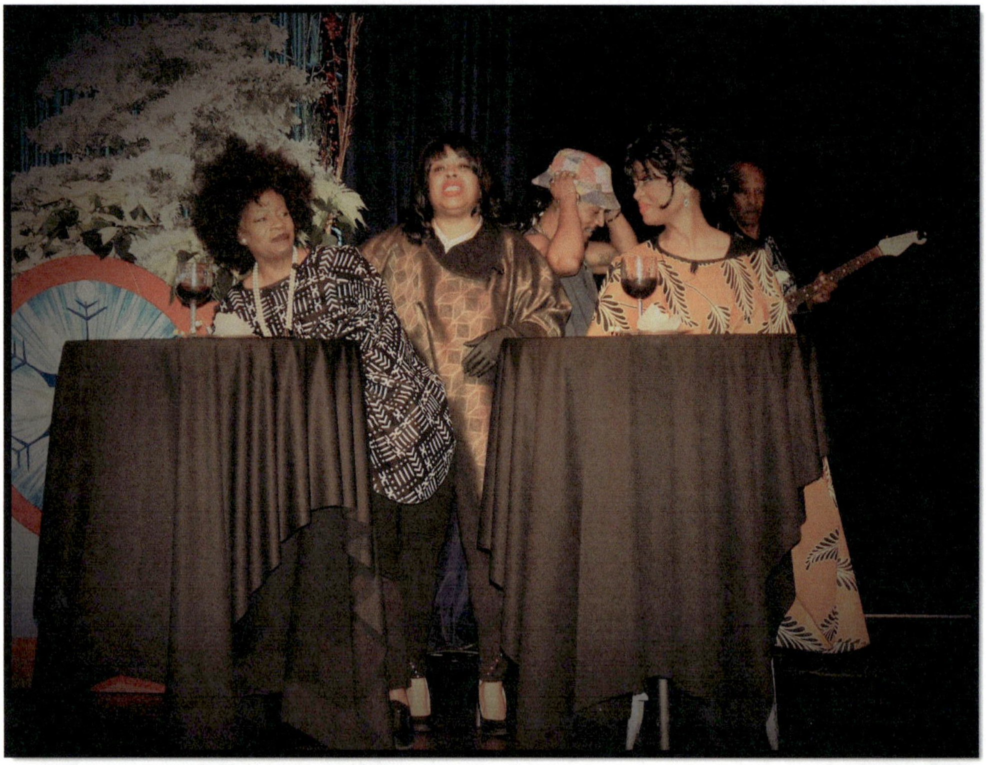

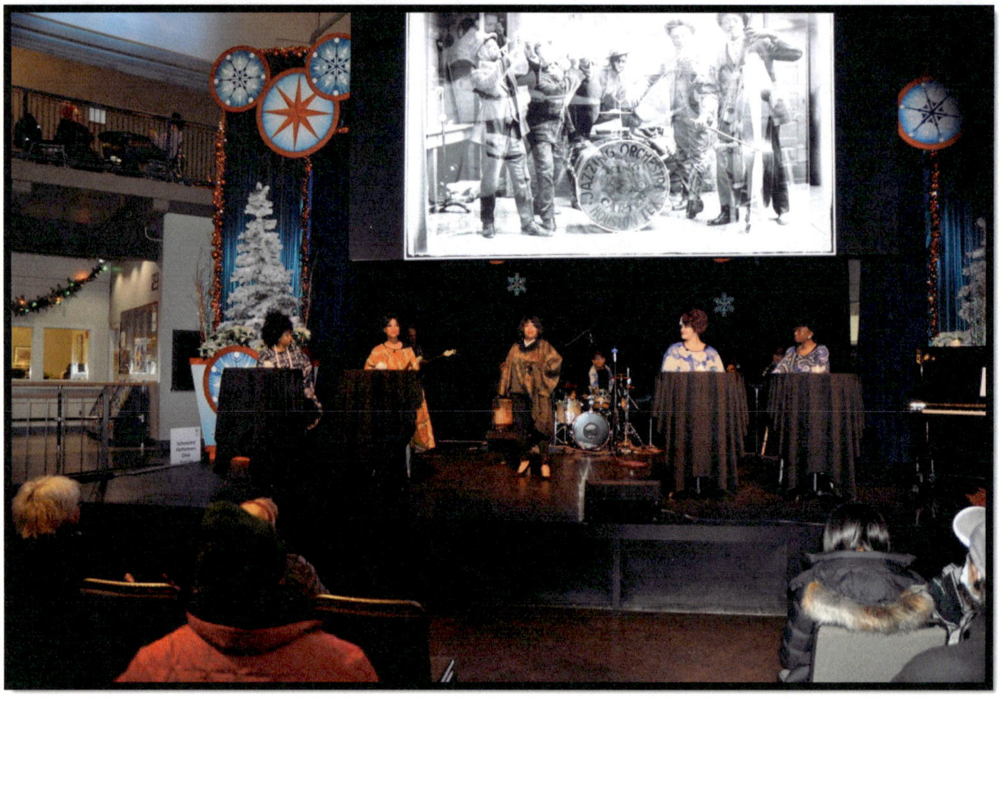

ONCE UPON A JAZZY SOUL AT THE JAM

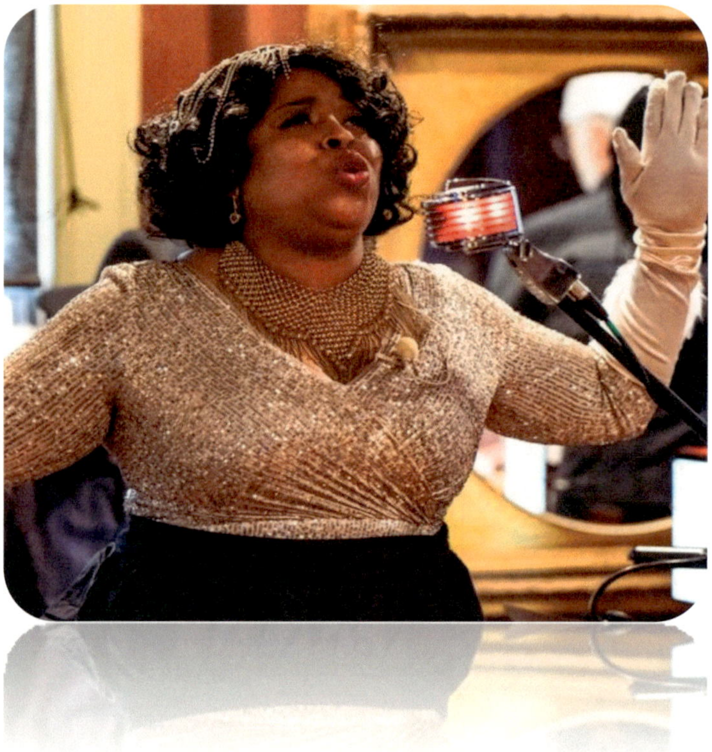

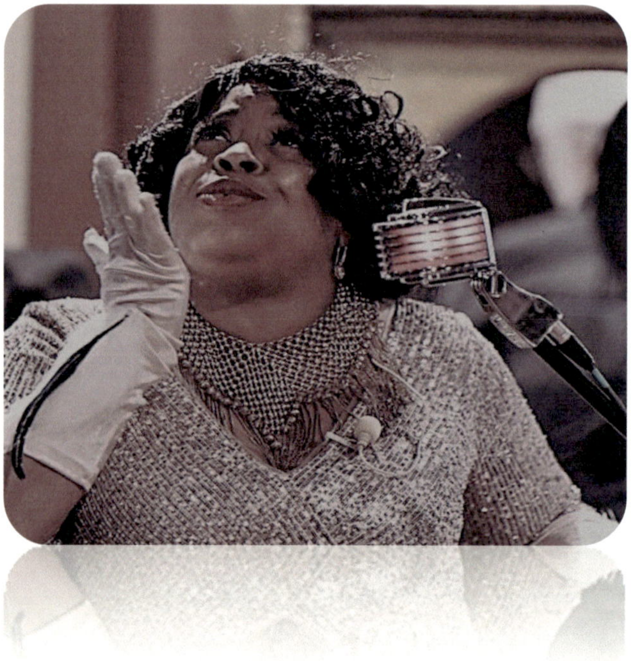

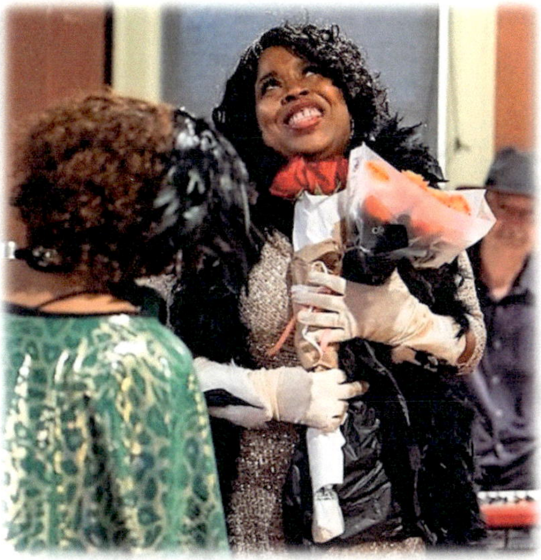

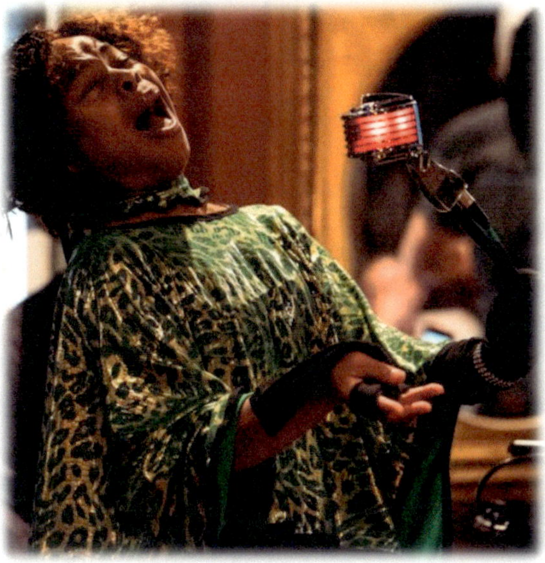

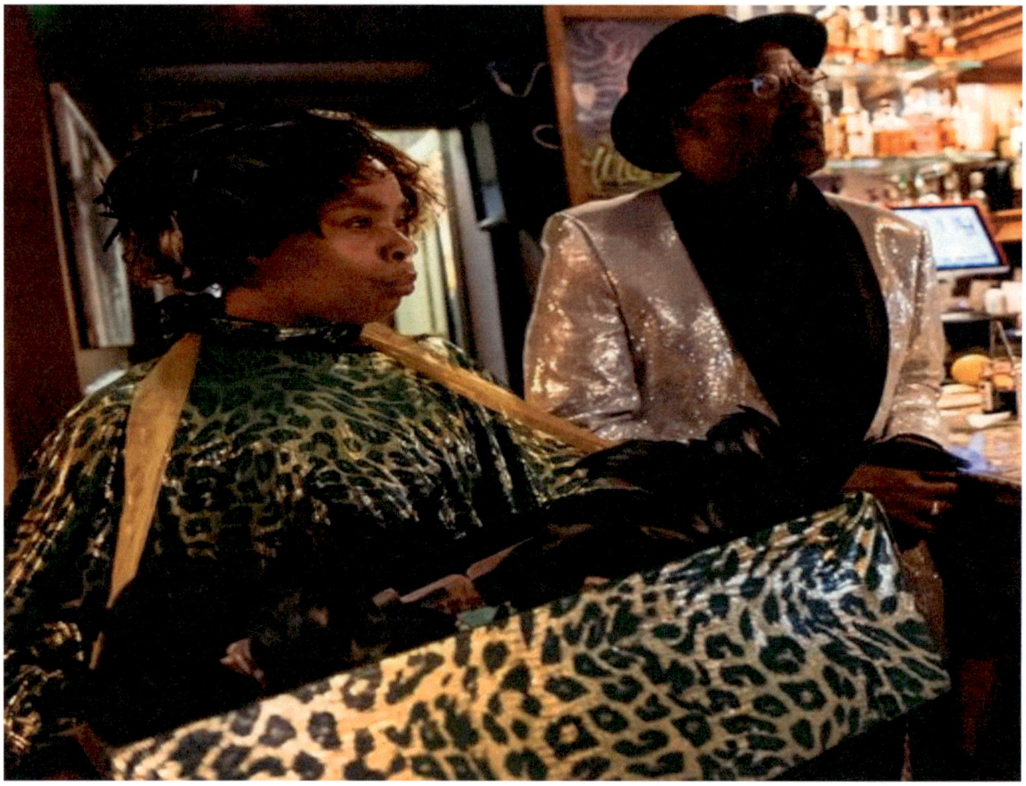

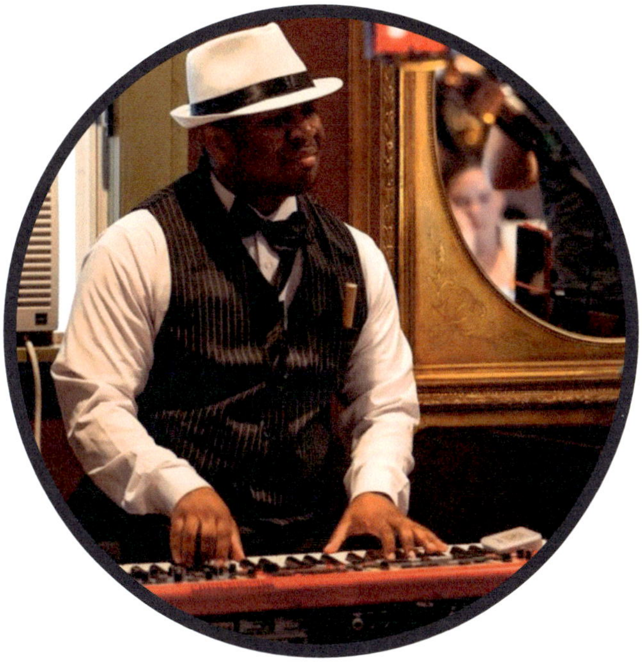

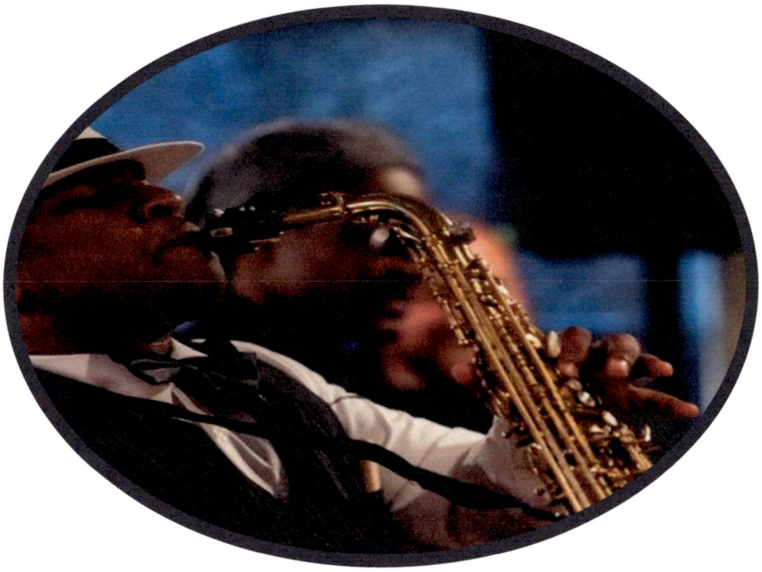

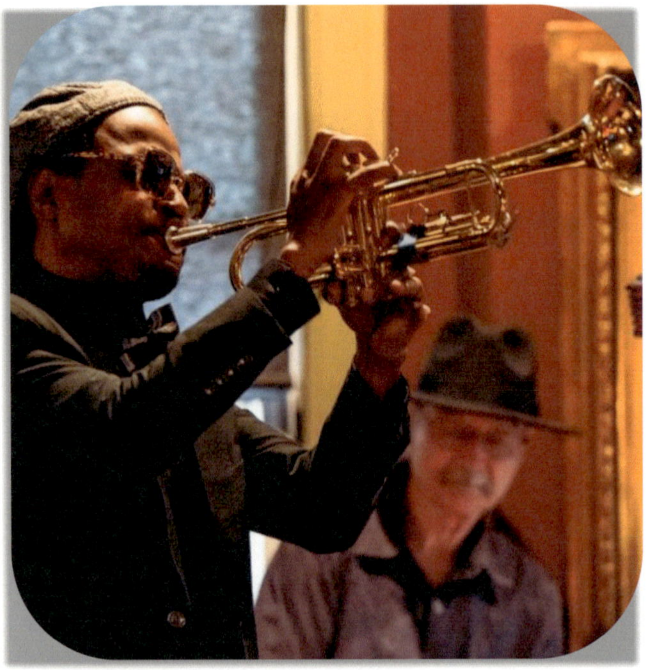

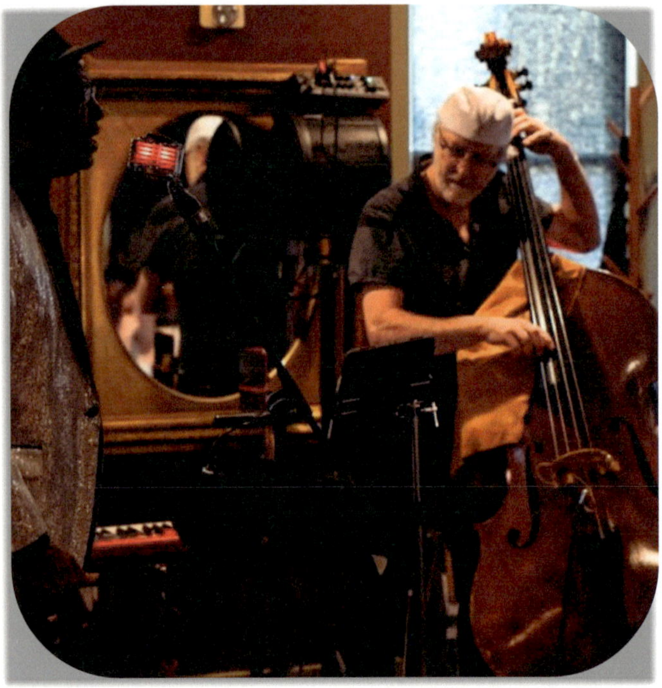

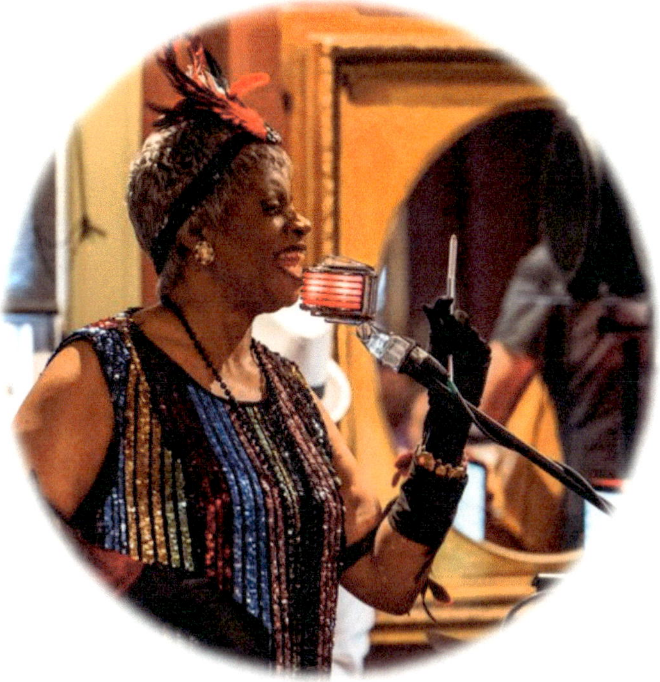

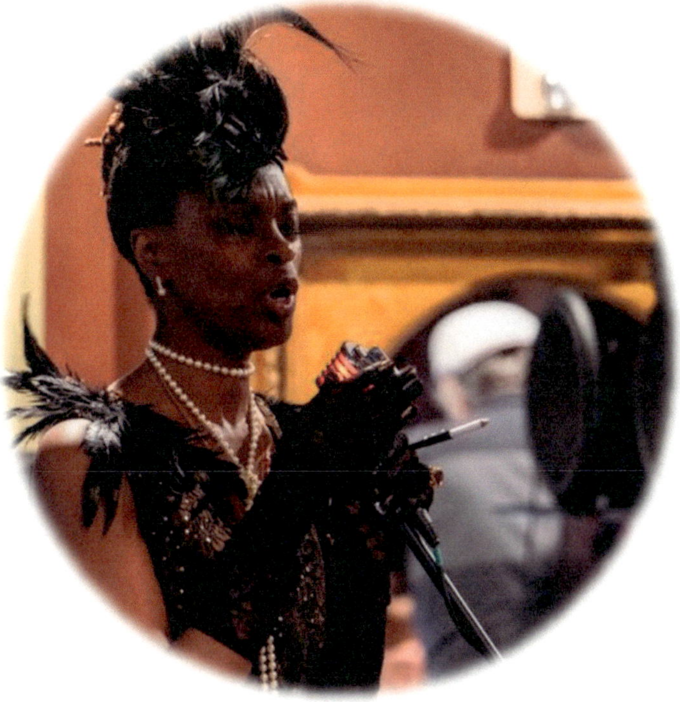

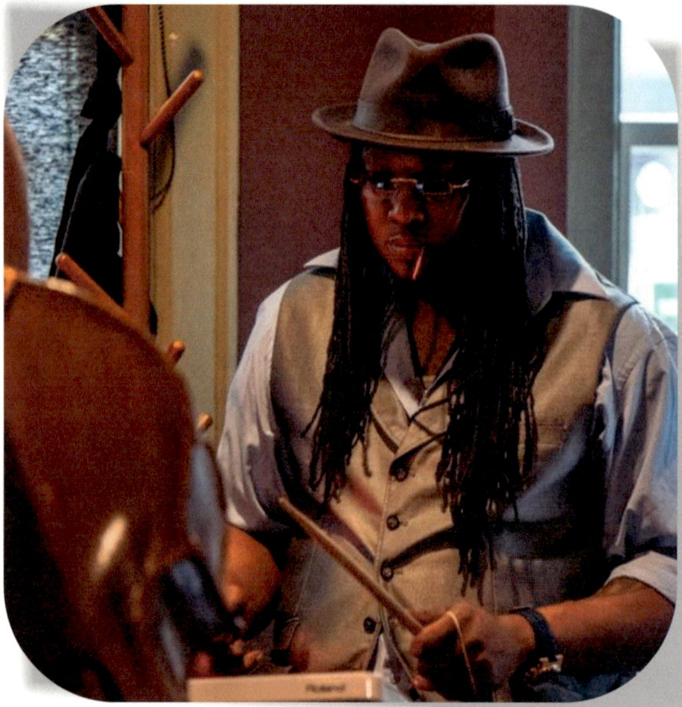

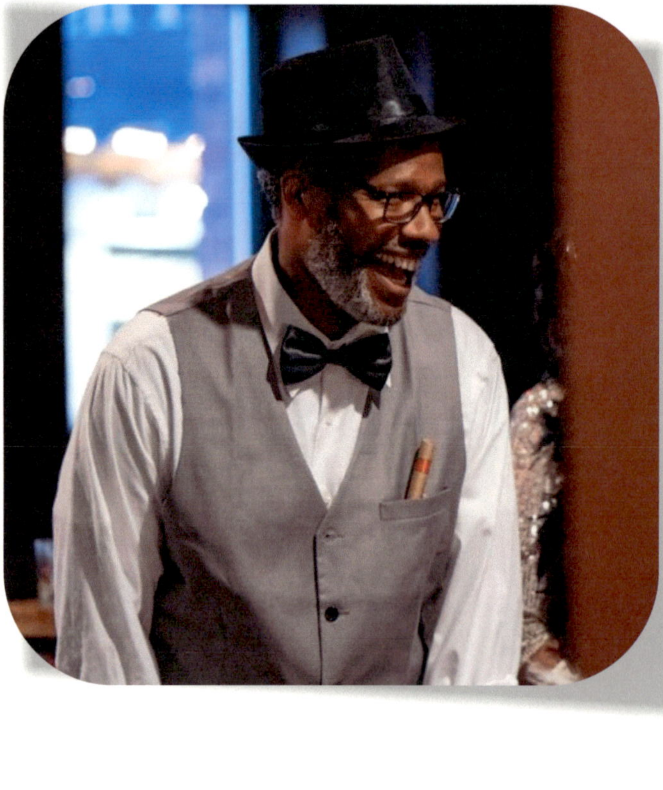

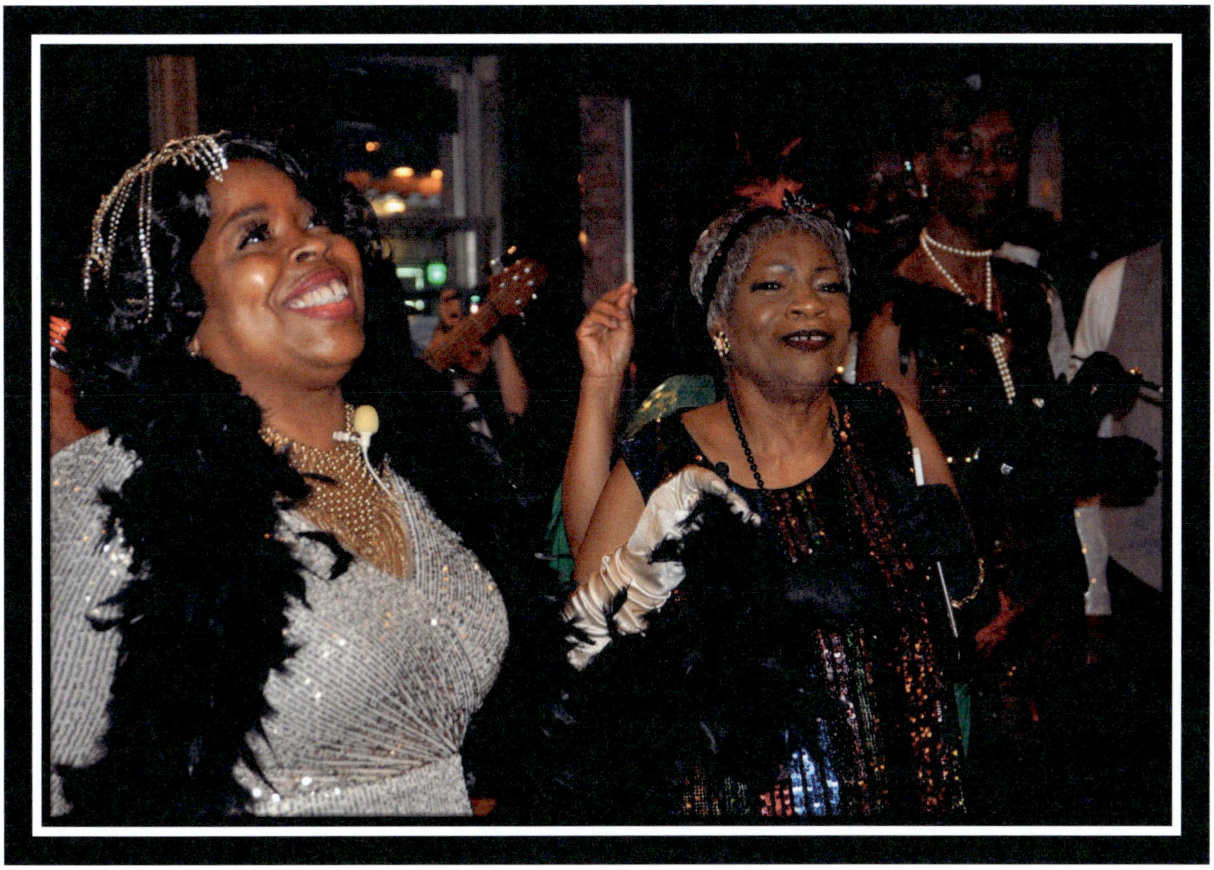

BLAQUE THEATER
Miz Portiontè Floes